sew zoey

LIGHTS, CAMERA, FASHION!

written by
Chloe Taylor

illustrated by
Nancy Zhang

Simon Spotlight

New York London Toronto Sydney New Delhi

This book is a work of fiction. Any references to historical events, real people, or real places are used fictitiously. Other names, characters, places, and events are the product of the author's imagination, and any resemblance to actual events or places or persons, living or dead, is entirely coincidental.

SIMON SPOTLIGHT
An imprint of Simon & Schuster Children's Publishing Division
1230 Avenue of the Americas, New York, New York 10020
Copyright © 2013 by Simon & Schuster, Inc.
All rights reserved, including the right of reproduction in
whole or in part in any form.
SIMON SPOTLIGHT and colophon are registered trademarks
of Simon & Schuster, Inc.
For information about special discounts for bulk purchases,
please contact Simon & Schuster Special Sales at 1-866-506-1949
or business@simonandschuster.com.
Text by Sarah Darer Littman
Manufactured in the United States of America 1013 OFF
First Edition 10 9 8 7 6 5 4 3 2
ISBN 978-1-4424-8979-0 (pbk)
ISBN 978-1-4424-8980-6 (hc)
ISBN 978-1-4424-8981-3 (eBook)
Library of Congress Catalog Card Number 2013935206

---------- CHAPTER 1 ----------

To Thine Own Self Be . . . Blue?

When I thought seventh grade would be so much better than sixth grade, I forgot that CERTAIN PEOPLE—mainly one certain person—would still think their job is to make life at Mapleton Prep difficult. Everyone always says you just have to ignore those people, but it's not easy, because they're in school every day. When I feel blue about it, Dad says I should follow Shakespeare's advice and "Above all, to thine own self be true," which is a fancy way of telling me to be myself and stop caring so much what everyone else thinks. It's easy for him to say—he's not in middle school.

Speaking of being true to yourself, Aunt Lulu took me to see a Frida Kahlo exhibit at the art museum over the weekend. Frida's life was so sad, but her art . . . WOW! It jumped off the walls and hit you in the face, as if it was saying, "This is me. Deal with it!" For a person who was often in pain, her paintings were bursting with energy.

Anyway, what I loved the most was that her self-portraits showed off her style: She mixed and matched bright colors, paired embroidered square tunics with lace-trimmed skirts, and wore flowers or ribbons in her hair (which kind of made it look like she was wearing a crown, at least to me.) I loved it all and would give just about anything to go shopping in her closet. And I totally want to wear flowers in my hair from now on. I did a sketch of a few outfits inspired by Frida's wardrobe with a silk flower, lace, and tons of embroidery. Maybe it seems like too much, but if I make it, I'll just wear it with confidence like Frida did.

I also want to go to Mexico someday to visit Frida Kahlo's house, *La Casa Azul*. There are so many places I want to go! But the only place I can go right now is to bed. Dad just shouted, "Lights out!" since it's a school night. Feeling less blue already! Thanks for listening.

xo,

Zoey

"I think you're going to love this one," Ms. Brown said, winking at Zoey Webber as she handed her a copy of what the class was going to read next. Zoey turned the book over. When she saw the title, *The Misfits*, her heart sank. English was her favorite class and her teacher, Ms. Brown, seemed to really understand her. Did Ms. Brown think she was a misfit? Not that she wanted to be just like everyone else, but . . . "misfit" implied there was something wrong with her, like she was an odd piece in a puzzle that would otherwise fit together perfectly.

Zoey turned to the description on the back of

the book. "Sticks and stones may break our bones but names will break our spirit." The synopsis said that the kids in the story wanted to be seen for who they really were inside, instead of "as the one-word jokes their classmates have tried to reduce them to."

Okay, maybe it's worth a try, she thought.

Just then the PA system hissed to life. "Good morning, Mapleton Prep students. This is Ms. Austen," the principal said through the loudspeaker. "I have a special announcement. We are having our first dance of the year in a few weeks! This time it's going to be a Sadie Hawkins dance."

From the murmurs of "What's that?" and "Sadie who?" Zoey could tell she wasn't the only one who didn't know what that meant, but Ms. Austen continued.

"A Sadie Hawkins dance is also called a Vice Versa dance, because instead of the boys asking the girls to the dance, it's vice versa. Ladies, this is your chance to do the asking, and, gentlemen, you can sit back, relax, and wait for your invitations. Tickets go on sale tomorrow."

The class erupted as soon as the announcement ended. Zoey wished she could talk to her friend Kate Mackey, but Kate was at a dentist appointment.

"Why do we have to wait for the girls to ask us?" Joe Latrone complained. "That's not fair!"

"Do we have to ask a boy?" Shannon Chang spoke up. "Can we just wait for them to ask us?"

"You don't *have* to ask a boy," Ms. Brown told her. "You can go with a group of friends. And, Joe, why is it any more fair for a girl to wait for you to ask her?"

"I don't know." Joe shrugged. "'That's how it happens."

"Yeah," Rob Palmer said. "It's how it's always been."

"Well, this time it'll happen differently," Ms. Brown said. "If we always stuck to the status quo, we'd still have slavery and women wouldn't have the vote. Sometimes change is good."

Ms. Brown started class, but as soon as they broke into their small-group discussions, talk turned to the dance and what to wear. Ivy Wallace was in the group next to Zoey's. Zoey heard her boasting that she had the perfect dress. Zoey wondered what that looked like.

Suddenly, Ivy turned around and said, "I bet *you're* going to turn up in one of those stupid craft projects from your blog. That'll attract a lot of dates!"

Zoey lifted her chin and tried to ignore Ivy and the giggles she heard from the other kids in Ivy's group, but Ivy's remark still hurt her just as much. She tried to remind herself of all the great comments she got about her designs from her blog readers.

"I'll go with Zoey."

It was Gabe Monaco, the guy who sat in front of her. Zoey didn't even know him that well. He was always nice to her, but it wasn't like they were friends or anything. And she didn't have a crush on him, the way she did on . . . someone else.

Zoey smiled. "Thanks. That's really nice of you."

"I mean it," he said.

"I know," Zoey said, but that just made her more confused. Was he just being nice because Ivy was

lights, camera, fashion!

being mean, or was he asking her? Wasn't this supposed to be a Vice Versa dance? She just smiled back at Gabe, unsure of what to say or do. Zoey never felt more saved by the bell than when it rang and she could escape to her next class.

When Zoey and her best friends, Kate Mackey, Priti Holbrooke, and Libby Flynn, met for lunch, the Sadie Hawkins dance was the number-one topic of conversation.

"Okay, we've got two important things to figure out," Priti announced. "Who to ask and what to wear."

"I have no idea who to ask," Libby said. "I don't have a crush on anyone."

"Not even the teensiest little hint of a crush?" Zoey asked.

"Nope," Libby said. "Not even a smidgen."

"Neither do I," Kate confessed. "I was thinking maybe I could ask someone from the soccer team. Or the swim team. You know, like, a guy friend."

"None of you have crushes?" Priti asked, amazed. "I have one, and I'm definitely asking him."

"Who?" Libby asked. "Spill!"

"Felix Egerton. He's in my social studies class, and he's soooo cute!"

"I know Felix," Kate said. "He's on the soccer team."

"Tell me *everything*!" Priti demanded. "What's he like?"

"Um . . . I guess he's nice. I don't really know him that well," Kate said. "Just from practice. We don't hang out or anything."

"Has he ever mentioned my name?" Priti asked.

Kate picked at her sandwich crust. "No, but . . . it's not like we talk that much, so I wouldn't take it as a sign of anything."

"What about you, Zoey?" Libby asked. "Do you have a wild crush you're dying to ask?"

"Well, I still kind of like, you know . . ." She paused, afraid to tell anyone, but these were her best friends, after all. "Here goes . . . I was thinking of asking . . . Lorenzo Romy."

"He's cute!" Priti said. "You should go for it!"

"I want to, but just the thought of going up and asking him makes me want to throw up," Zoey confessed. "And that wouldn't make him want to go with me, would it?"

"Um, no!" Libby giggled. "That would be a deal breaker."

"Let's talk about something more fun, like what we're going to wear," Zoey said, because thinking about asking Lorenzo was making her queasy.

"I don't have a date, but I have a dress," Libby said. "I'm going to wear that awesometastic pink ruffled birthday-cake dress Zoey made me."

It gave Zoey the warm fuzzies knowing Libby loved the dress she made so much that she wanted to wear it to the dance.

"At least *you* don't think my designs are 'stupid craft projects.'" She sighed.

Her friends all stared at her like she had suddenly dyed her hair magenta.

"Why would I think *that*?" Libby asked.

"I know, right? That's totally crazy," Priti said.

Zoey told them about what Ivy said in English.

"Oh, Zo, don't let *Ivy* get to you," Kate said.

"I know," Zoey said. "I should ignore her. But how come the bad stuff people say always sticks in your head more than the good things?"

"Good question," Priti said. "But if it makes you feel any better, I'd love nothing better than to go to the dance with Felix in an original design by Sew Zoey."

"Me too," Kate said. "Except not with Felix, obviously."

"I'd love to design dresses for you!" Zoey exclaimed.

As soon as Zoey started thinking about designs for her friends, Ivy's comments didn't seem to matter as much.

"It's all settled, then," Priti said. "Now the rest of you just have to figure out who to ask. It's as simple as that."

Zoey wished it *were* as simple as that. Designing dresses wasn't simple, but it was something she was comfortable doing. Asking a boy to a dance? Well, that was another story. . . .

------------ CHAPTER 2 ------------

Kate's Date with Fate

Guess what? We've got a dance coming up and get this: It's a Sadie Hawkins, or Vice Versa, dance, which means the *girls* have to ask the *boys*. I know, right? It's bad enough having to worry if someone is going to ask you, but now I have to the asking. If you're wondering, yes, I have someone in mind to ask, but no, I haven't gotten up the courage yet. It's easier to think about fun stuff like designing dresses for my friends to wear.

I've attached a sketch of ideas for Kate's dress. I want to make something really pretty, but not in a flashy way—just like her. Also, I want to make it a shape and material that's easy to wear, since she's not big on dresses. Maybe sparkle-dotted tulle would be just enough to make it feel special without being too much for her.

What did you wear to your middle school dance? And while I'm asking questions, I might as well ask the one thing I *really* want to know: Did you ever ask out a boy? How did you do it? Was it really awkward? Every time I think about asking You Know Who—well, okay, You *Don't* Know Who ☺—it makes my tummy churn like a washer on the spin cycle. See, there it goes right now! I'd better start thinking about something safer, like the dress I'm going to design for Priti!

"Have you asked anyone yet?" Priti said as the girls walked into The Perfect Ten nail salon for a mani-pedi treat. Libby shot her a look. "Not in front of my mom!" she hissed.

"I heard nothing. I'm hard of hearing in that ear," Libby's mom said, her lips twitching. "I'll go find myself a magazine and be hard of hearing somewhere else."

"Great idea, Mom," Libby said. "We'll pick our polish."

As usual, Zoey and Libby headed for the bright colors, Priti gravitated to the glitter, and Kate made a beeline for the pale pink section since they looked the most natural.

"Do you think this one clashes with my hair?" Libby asked, holding up a bottle of red polish.

"Ooh!" Zoey exclaimed. "There was an article in *Très Chic* about redheads! It said you should hold the bottle up to the inside of your wrist to see if it matches your skin tone."

Libby held the nail polish to her wrist. "Sooo . . . what does that tell me?"

"It looks good to me," Zoey said.

"If Sew Zoey says it doesn't clash, that's all I need to know," Libby said.

Zoey picked a fluorescent lime-green shade called Gargantuan Green Grape.

"Wow, that's really bright," Kate said. She was holding a bottle of pale pink polish.

"Do you think my nails will look big in it?" Zoey joked.

"Oh no!" Kate said, afraid she'd offended Zoey. She rolled the bottle of polish in her hand. "It's just . . . you know me. I don't like to stand out."

"That's why you have to try something new instead of the same pink," Priti argued. "You need to step it up a little, girl." She picked up bottle of fuchsia. "Here. Pink Before You Leap. It's perfect."

Kate's eyes widened in horror. "Perfect for you, maybe. It's too . . ." Her voice trailed off.

Zoey knew Kate was trying to figure out a way to say why it wasn't right for her without hurting Priti's feelings. "Priti, you know Kate only likes to stand out on the sports field."

"You're right." Priti shrugged, picking up a sparkly silver polish that looked like the inside of a snow globe. "I guess she wouldn't be cool with Glitzerland, either."

Kate shook her head.

"Is the skiing good in Glitzerland?" Libby asked.

"OMG, it's the best," Priti said. "Because when you wipe out, everything sparkles."

They were all giggling as they walked back to the pedicure chairs. Once they were settled, Priti looked around to make sure Libby's mother was out of earshot.

"Okay, so . . . has anyone asked a date to the dance yet?"

Kate looked down at her toes. Libby looked at the ceiling. Zoey inspected her nails.

"I haven't. Just thinking about it makes me feel sick," Zoey said.

"I haven't either," Libby confessed.

"That makes three of us." Kate sighed.

"Well, I'm going to ask Felix first thing on Monday because I don't want anyone else to ask him first," Priti said. Zoey couldn't believe how confident she sounded about the whole thing. "And you guys should hurry up and ask too so we all have someone to go with."

"How am I supposed to hurry up and ask when I

have no idea *who* to ask?" Libby groaned.

"There's got to be *someone*," Priti insisted.

"Nope. There isn't." Libby said.

"I'm in the same boat," Kate said. "I don't really *like* anyone."

"I just don't know how to ask Lorenzo," Zoey admitted.

"Walk up to him, hopefully when he's alone, and say, 'Lorenzo, do you want to go to the dance with me?'" Priti suggested.

Zoey, Libby, and Kate exchanged glances. They all loved Priti, but there were times when she just didn't seem to get that they weren't as confident as she was.

"He's never alone. Maybe if I had his cell number, I could text him, but I don't. Maybe you could feel him out for me," Zoey said to Priti.

"I guess I could," Priti said.

"Do you think anyone will break the rules?" Kate asked.

"What do you mean?" Libby said.

"I mean, a boy asking a girl, even though it's a Vice Versa dance," Kate explained.

"You know what they say: Rules are made to be broken," Priti said. "But I think it's safer to ask rather than wait to be asked. Besides, it's a Vice Versa dance. That's part of the fun."

"I know," Kate said. "But I still wish I didn't have to ask anyone."

"Me too." Libby sighed.

"I don't think that part's fun at all," Zoey said.

"Come on, you guys!" Priti said. "Didn't you read the comments on Zoey's blog? Lots of people asked out boys in high school."

"Yeah, and a few of them said it was the most mortifying experience *ever*!" Zoey said.

"How are the pedicures going?" Mrs. Flynn stopped to check on them on the way to get her manicure. Zoey was grateful for the interruption. Anything to change the subject!

Zoey could hear the crash and beat of Marcus practicing his drums in the basement when she walked into the house. She headed down and sat on the bottom step, waiting for the end of the song.

"What's up, Zo?"

She held up her hands. "What do you think?"

"If we have a power outage, I'll just look for your nails," Marcus said, grinning.

"Can I ask you a question?"

"As long as it's not about nail polish."

Zoey told Marcus about the Vice Versa dance. "There's this guy I want to ask, but . . . every time I think about asking him, I feel like I'm going to throw up. So I figured since you're, you know, a *guy*, you could give me some advice."

Marcus threw his drumsticks into the air and caught them. "Well . . . number one, don't giggle. There's nothing worse than a girl who giggles all the time. So annoying."

"Okay, no giggling. Anything else?"

Marcus pondered. "Oh! Don't get someone else to ask if he likes you or to ask him to the dance for you."

Uh-oh . . .

"Why not get someone to find out if he likes you if it saves humiliation?" Zoey asked.

"Because everyone ends up knowing, and then there's all this drama," Marcus said.

"Hello? Anyone home?"

"Down here, Dad!" Marcus shouted.

Mr. Webber's feet appeared first, followed by the rest of him. His cheeks were ruddy after being outside at the Eastern State University football game. He was the university's head physical therapist, so he went to most of their games.

"Did you win?" Zoey asked.

"Not this time. Got beat 38–17." Her dad sighed. "Defense was half asleep today."

Zoey hugged her father. "There's always next weekend."

"True. I'll make sure to bring them a Box of Joe before the game next week," he said. "So what are you two plotting down here?"

"Nothing," Zoey said.

"Zo wanted to know how to ask out a boy," Marcus said, ignoring his sister's *don't tell Dad* look.

Mr. Webber sank onto the old, worn sofa they kept down in the basement for when Marcus's friends came over to jam.

"I'm not ready for this," he said. "Besides, isn't the boy supposed to ask out the girl?"

"It's a Sadie Hawkins dance," Zoey explained. "Everything is vice versa."

"What has Mr. Dear Abby told you so far?" Mr. Webber asked.

"Don't ask anyone to ask the guy if he likes me or to ask him to the dance for me." Zoey sighed. "Which stinks, because that's what I was planning to do."

Her father patted the sofa. Zoey sat down next to him. He put his arm around her.

"Honey, having a relationship means taking risks with your ego, but most of all with your heart. Sure, you get hurt sometimes, but when you meet the right person, it's just . . . the most incredible feeling in the world."

"Like it was with Mom?" Zoey asked, leaning her head against her father's shoulder.

She felt his sharp intake of breath. Maybe she shouldn't have brought up her mom.

But then her father stroked her hair gently. "Yes, honey, like it was with your mom."

He picked up her hand. "Wow, Zo, your nails are very . . . green."

"They're not just green," Zoey said. "They're Gargantuan Green."

"More like Nuclear Meltdown Green," Marcus said.

"Dad . . . do *you* have any advice?" Zoey asked.

Her father closed his eyes for a moment. When he opened them, they were glistening.

"Zoey, if I had my way, my advice would be to stay my little girl forever."

"Daaaad . . ."

"I know, I know, that's not an option. So my advice to you, Zo, is just be yourself. And if the kid is too dumb to say yes, that's his loss."

"Dad's right, Zo," Marcus said, "Be cool."

Somehow, Zoey didn't feel any better about the thought of asking Lorenzo, because if there was one thing she *wasn't*, it was "cool."

"I like your nails," Lorenzo said before social studies class started. "Cool color."

"Um . . . thanks," Zoey said. "My brother said it looked radioactive, but I like it."

Lorenzo laughed. "Now that I think about it . . ."

"I like bright, cheerful things," Zoey said.

"I can tell by your clothes," Lorenzo said, grinning.

Just then Mr. Dunn started class, leaving Zoey to wonder if Lorenzo thought that was a good thing—and to summon up the courage to pop the dance question after class.

She kept rehearsing different versions in her head of how to ask Lorenzo out. When Mr. Dunn called on her, she had to ask him to repeat the question.

"What is the teaching style pioneered by a philosopher in ancient Greece?"

Luckily, Zoey remembered the answer. "The Socratic method."

Mr. Dunn looked at her over the top of his glasses. "Correct, Miss Webber, but I'd appreciate it if you paid attention."

Zoey heard snickering from the back of the room, where Ivy, Shannon, and Bree Sharpe were sitting. She was embarrassed and flustered—about as far from cool as she could possibly be. But Priti was expecting her to ask Lorenzo today, and Zoey wasn't sure which was worse: asking Lorenzo or facing a disappointed Priti.

Zoey was beginning to wish they'd just cancel the dance. Well, not really, because then she wouldn't be able to make the amazing dresses she was designing for her friends—and maybe for herself, if she ever got a date.

When the bell rang, she picked up her books and tried to maneuver herself next to Lorenzo as he walked out of the room so she could try to get him alone. But just as she was within a foot of him, Ivy pushed past her, almost knocking Zoey off balance.

"Hey, Renzo!" she said. "Are you walking to lunch?"

Lorenzo shrugged. "Uh, yeah."

"Me too," Ivy simpered. She put her hand on his arm. "Come on—let's go."

Bree and Shannon followed behind Ivy and Lorenzo. Zoey's shoulders slumped. How was she *ever* going to get Lorenzo alone to ask him to the dance?

"Did you ask him?" Priti demanded before Zoey even sat down at the lunch table.

"No." Zoey sighed. "I tried. I spent the whole period psyching myself up to do it."

"What happened?" Priti asked.

"I was trying to get him alone, and then guess who barged in?" Zoey asked.

"I bet I know," Libby said. "Ivy."

Zoey nodded. "We were talking before class," she said. "He said he liked my nail polish."

"He noticed your nail polish? That's a good sign!" Priti said.

"Maybe," Kate said. She'd already taken hers off.

"Definitely," Libby said.

Zoey felt a little more hopeful. Maybe she'd get a chance to ask Lorenzo tomorrow. Or the day after that. If Ivy didn't ask him first.

Mrs. Holbrooke dropped off Priti at Zoey's house later that afternoon on her way to pick up Tara and Sashi, Priti's sisters, from the high school. "I won't be long," she warned. "Be ready to leave when I get back."

As soon as her mother started backing out of the driveway, Priti grabbed Zoey's arm and whispered, "GUESS WHAT?!"

"What?" Zoey asked. "And can you let go of my arm before it falls off from lack of circulation?"

"Oh sorry," Priti said. "But . . . Felix said *yes*!"

"Wow!" Zoey exclaimed. "Tell me *everything*!"

They flopped onto the sofa in the living room.

"So . . . how did you ask him? What did he say?"

"I walked up to him, made a little small talk about homework, and then asked him if he wanted to go to the dance. And he said yes. Well . . . actually he said, 'Sure.'"

"It's the same thing, pretty much," Zoey said.

"You *have* to invite Lorenzo now, Zo! And we need to find someone for Libby. And Kate . . . I don't understand her. She's so pretty, she could ask anyone, but she doesn't seem to care."

Talking about the date situation just made Zoey's stomach twist into knots again. Luckily, she knew how to get Priti to change the subject.

"So, do you have any ideas about your dress?" she asked.

"Oh yeah!" Priti said, her eyes lighting up.

"Let's go upstairs," Zoey suggested. "I can start sketching out some designs."

"Yes!" Priti said. "I'm thinking sequins. Lots of sequins! With a V neck and a scoop back."

Sketching for Priti was so different from designing for Kate, because Priti had such definite ideas about what she wanted.

"No, not like that," she said, pointing to the fall of the skirt Zoey had sketched. "A bit shorter. But not too short or Mom will freak out."

Zoey erased yet another line. She was almost relieved when the doorbell rang and Marcus called up the stairs that Mrs. Holbrooke was back to pick up Priti. It was easier for her to get ideas on paper first, and then let everyone make suggestions.

As soon as Priti left, Zoey sketched out a few more ideas for her friend. Then she turned to a fresh page, blank with possibility, and tried to envision her own dress. But doing that made her think about having a date . . . and about asking Lorenzo. Sighing, she closed her sketchbook and decided to do homework instead.

-------- CHAPTER 3 ---------

A Pretty Dress for Priti!

Guess what? My friend Priti came over yesterday and told me . . . she has a date to the dance! We got right down to business, a.k.a. what to wear! I sketched out a few dresses (all of which involved sequins, because Priti loves to sparkle), but this one is the main contender.

Now I just have to get sewing. Gosh! Sewing on all those sequins is going to take forever. Hopefully, it'll be worth it: Her dream dress for her dream date!

The thing is, now that Priti has a date, I can't keep avoiding the Big Ask. It's my turn, and the clock is ticking.

I almost asked You Don't Know Who yesterday, but it didn't happen. I guess I'm scared! I've been distracting myself by reading *The Misfits* by James Howe for English. Bobby, the narrator, wonders if when they graduate and go out into the Grown-Up World, it won't be him and the other Misfits who feel out of place, but the kids who are making their lives miserable. He wonders if the rest of the world outside of middle school and high school is made up of people who are called misfits because "they're just who they are instead of 'fits' like everybody else." I can't stop thinking about that. I wonder if that's true.

One thing that is a misfit: the zipper on Kate's dress! I must have measured wrong because it kept puckering. I had to redo it *five times*. And here I thought Kate's dress was going to be the easy one! Well, gotta run. Wish me luck with You Don't Know Who!

"Does it ever get old, working in this amazing store?" Zoey asked Jan, the owner of A Stitch in Time. She'd begged Aunt Lulu to bring her to buy fabric for Priti's dress.

Jan propped her rainbow-striped glasses up into her long dark hair. "Never. Especially when I have fun customers like you."

"Every time I come in, it's like walking into a cave of buried treasure." Zoey sighed. "I want to buy *everything*."

Aunt Lulu chuckled. "Well, since you're on a budget, Zo, let's focus on what you *need*."

"I know," Zoey said, taking the list out of her pocket.

Jan lowered her reading glasses onto the end of her nose and took the list. "So which designs did you go with?"

Zoey still couldn't believe Jan read Sew Zoey and recommended it to her customers.

Zoey flipped open her sketchbook and showed Jan the design Priti picked for her dress.

"Stunning," Jan said. "You're crazy talented."

"That's what I tell her," Aunt Lulu agreed.

Zoey felt like the sun was beaming from her chest. If Lorenzo walked into A Stitch in Time (as if!), she would walk right up to him and ask him if he wanted to go to the dance.

Jan helped her pick out the best value fabric, and then they went to the huge wall of sequins and accessories.

"You can buy this stretch sequin trim instead of sewing each one on individually," Jan suggested. "It'll save you a lot of time."

"Great!" Zoey said. She was already worrying about getting her friends' dresses made before the dance and still having enough time to create something amazing for herself.

As if she could read Zoey's mind, Jan asked, "So when are you going to show me the fabulous dress you've designed for yourself?"

Zoey looked down at her Converse sneakers. "I . . . um . . . haven't made it yet."

"Why not, honey?" Aunt Lulu asked.

"Because I haven't got a date," Zoey mumbled.

"You haven't asked the Mystery Man?" Jan said.

"No," Zoey said mournfully. "Just thinking about it makes me feel sick."

"Honey, sometimes you just have to fake it till you make it," Aunt Lulu said. "I'll be really nervous about getting a big client, but I won't show it." She put her arm across Zoey's shoulders and gave her a quick hug. "I walk in there and act confident, like I believe I'm the best person in the whole world for the job, even though I've got butterflies in my stomach and pray they don't see my knees shaking."

"Really?" Zoey said. She couldn't imagine Lulu being scared of anything.

"You bet. And you know what? After a few minutes, I don't just fool my client into believing I'm confident, I even fool myself."

"It's all up here," Jan said, tapping Zoey's forehead gently with her finger. "I want you to go home and design yourself something totally *Très Chic*–worthy. The trim is on me. "

"Thank you!" Zoey exclaimed, giving Jan a hug.

"On one condition. On Monday, I want you to march right up to Mystery Man and ask him to the dance. Deal?"

Jan stuck out her hand. Zoey took it and shook. "It's a deal."

As soon as Aunt Lulu dropped her off at home, Zoey raced up to her room and curled up on her bed with her sketchbook and pencils. Now that she had a plan to ask Lorenzo to the dance, it was time to imagine the perfect dress. Her pencil hovered above the page, but . . . nothing. Usually she couldn't sketch fast enough to keep up with all the ideas in her head. After twenty minutes of frustration, she snapped her sketchbook shut and went over to her sewing table to start work on Priti's dress. At least her *friends* would have fabulous dresses.

When the phone rang in the middle of dinner, Marcus said, "I'll get it."

"Yeah, Zoey's here," he said. "Who did you say was calling again?"

Zoey almost choked on her lasagna. Could it be Lorenzo, asking her to the dance?

"Hey, Zo—it's some lady named Rashida Clarke. She's the producer of *Fashion Showdown*."

"*Seriously?*" Zoey exclaimed, jumping up so quickly, her chair fell over backward. "Why is she calling *me*?!"

"I don't know," Marcus said, his hand over the mouth of the phone. "Why don't you talk to her and find out?"

"*Fashion Showdown?*" her father asked. "That reality show you watch?"

Zoey nodded excitedly as she took the phone.

"Hi, this is Zoey." She was barely able to breathe.

"Zoey, so happy to reach you. My name is Rashida Clarke, and I'm the producer of *Fashion Showdown*, a reality show about—"

"I *love Fashion Showdown*," Zoey said. "I watch it all the time!"

"Terrific!" Rashida said. "The reason I'm calling is that we've seen your blog, and we're very impressed with it and your designs. We'd like to ask you to be a guest judge on the next episode of the show. It's a challenge to design dresses for a high school prom, so we want a teenage judge who knows more about fashion than the average teen on the street."

Zoey was speechless. It was a dream come true.

"Are you still there? I know this is very last minute—our original judge was a high school designer, but she had to back out."

"Yes . . . I'm here. And I'd love to do it. Just . . ." Zoey wanted to do the show more than anything. But she had to tell Rashida the truth. "The thing is, I'm not in high school. I'm only in seventh grade."

She held her breath, waiting, hoping that being in middle school wouldn't be the end of her shot at stardom.

"Don't worry about that, Zoey. You'll be terrific," Rashida said. "I've read your blog, and you've got a better design eye than people twice your age. You'll be doing us a huge favor by stepping in at the last minute like this."

Zoey exhaled. She couldn't believe that this was really happening—that she would be going to New York City to be a guest judge on *Fashion Showdown*!

Rashida was telling her all the details, but Zoey was too excited to take in any of it.

"Can I speak with your mom?"

It was as if Rashida had thrown a bucket of cold water through the phone receiver.

"Um . . . my mom . . . isn't . . . here. You can speak to my dad, though."

Her father gave her shoulder a gentle squeeze as he took the phone from her hand. It wasn't Rashida's fault. She didn't know. Most of the time Zoey was okay with it. But when people asked to speak to her mom, it reminded her of what she was missing.

"So what's this all about, Zo?" Marcus asked.

"Oh nothing," Zoey said. "Just that I'VE BEEN ASKED TO BE A JUDGE ON *FASHION SHOWDOWN*! ON TV!"

She danced around the kitchen while her father wrote down notes on a pad.

"Cool!" Marcus said. "My little sister, the TV star."

"If you load the dishwasher, I might just give you my autograph," Zoey said.

Her father hung up.

"Dad, I hate to break it to you, but Zoey's already turning into a diva," Marcus said.

Zoey's father wrapped her in a big bear hug that lifted her off her feet.

"My little girl, a TV star!" he said. "I'm so proud of you!"

"I won't be on TV if you break my ribs," Zoey squeaked.

Her father set her back on the floor. "Sorry, sweetheart." His warm hand rested gently on Zoey's cheek. "Mom would have been dancing around the kitchen with you."

There it was again. Zoey hated that empty space beneath her ribs.

"So what's the deal?" Marcus asked. "And when am I going to see my sister's face on the flat screen? Hey, Zo, I'll lend you my zit cream."

"Oh, thanks a lot, Marcus!" Zoey said. "I hadn't even thought about having a zit on TV. Now I'm going to worry so much, I'll probably get one!"

"Calm down," her dad said. "Even if you *do* get one, the show's makeup artist will cover it up. No one will see it."

"Even in high definition?" Zoey asked.

"Even in HD," her father reassured her. "As for seeing Zoey's face on the flat screen, they're going to call me back with all the travel details for the trip to New York. Until it's finalized, we have to keep this between us."

New York! One of the top fashion capitals of the world. And Zoey wasn't just going to be there. She was going to be a guest judge on *Fashion Showdown*!

"There's one problem. They want you there Thursday night because they start taping really early on Friday. I don't know if I can get off Thursday, because we have a game."

"What about Aunt Lulu?" Zoey asked. *Fashion Showdown* was one of the reality shows she and Aunt Lulu loved to watch together. A trip to the Big Apple to see the sights—and the stores—would be a lot of fun with her aunt.

"Good idea. *Fashion Showdown* is probably more up her alley."

"I could take Zoey," Marcus offered. "I'd love an all-expenses-paid trip to New York. I've always wanted to check out the music venues."

"Sorry, kiddo. Zoey's chaperone has to be an adult, eighteen or older," his father said.

"Why is everyone so ageist?" Marcus complained. "It's not fair."

"You focus on taking your upcoming driving test," Mr. Webber said. "I'll call Aunt Lulu to see if she's free to take Zoey."

Zoey felt like she was being carried up to her bedroom on a shining cloud instead of her Converse-shod feet. She closed the door and walked over to the full-length mirror to stare at her reflection. She looked like the same old Zoey, which made it hard to believe this was really happening.

Still, she couldn't help letting out an excited giggle and giving her mirror self a high five.

She was dying to tell Kate, Priti, and Libby, but what if it really *was* too good to be true? What if it turned out to be a great big mistake and Rashida Clarke called back to say they didn't want her on the show?

Zoey decided it was better to follow Rashida's rules and keep the secret under wraps until everything was confirmed, even though she felt like she was about to explode from keeping it.

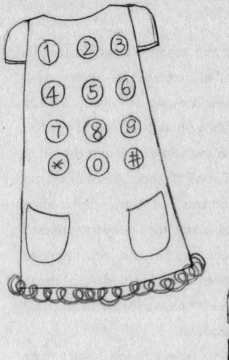

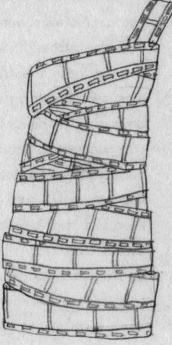

CHAPTER 4

Bursting at the Seams!!!

OMG, you guys! The MOST AMAZING THING IN THE ENTIRE WORLD HAS HAPPENED! There's just one teensy-weensy problem: I can't tell you what it is yet, or else I won't be allowed to be a part of the secret at all. This is torture! I want to tell you everything right now.

So I don't burst at the seams, I'm going to give you some clues about the secret, using—what else?—clothing sketches! It's Sew Zoey, right? Anyway, the first dress includes a hint about how I learned about this most awesome thing in the first place, and the other dress is a hint about what it's all about. You can tell me your guesses in the comments, but I can neither confirm nor deny if you're right. Sorry, they're not my rules! I know it's mean, but seriously, this is a hard secret to keep, and I would tell everybody if I could. And I mean *everybody*. Maybe I wouldn't have a hard time at school if certain people knew about it. . . .

But since I can't write about it and I can't think about anything else, I'm going to stop blogging for the moment. Just stay tuned, okay? Big news will be coming soon. Unless it's all a dream, in which case I don't want to wake up!

Sitting next to Kate on the bus the following Monday morning proved too much for Zoey's secret-keeping skills.

"You will never in a gazillion years guess what happened," Zoey said in a low voice.

Kate's eyes widened. "Did Lorenzo ask you to the dance?"

The thought of the dance and her lack of a date for it put a momentary damper on Zoey's excitement.

"No. And I haven't asked him yet, either, in case that's what you were going to ask next."

"So . . . what is it? Tell me!"

Zoey told Kate about the phone call from Rashida Clarke.

"*You're going to be on TV?!*" Kate squeaked.

"Shh!" Zoey hissed. "It's a secret, remember?"

"That's so amazing, Zo!" Kate said. "And they found you through Sew Zoey!"

"I know. Who would have thought a little blog could lead to being on TV?"

"We have to have a watch party when the episode airs. It'll be so much fun!"

"If it happens," Zoey said. "I checked the notepad by the phone this morning to make sure my dad really had written down the producer's details, because I was afraid I'd dreamed the whole thing."

"Why wouldn't it happen?" Kate asked.

"I don't know. Maybe they'll decide they really do want someone who's in high school. It *is* a *high school* prom dress challenge, after all."

"They won't do that," Kate said. "They wouldn't have asked you if they didn't really want you."

"I guess. It's just hard to believe that they'd want me, Zoey Webber, seventh grader at Mapleton Prep, to be a judge on *Fashion Showdown*."

"Why not?" Kate patted Zoey's knee comfortingly. "Coach says, 'If you think you can't, you won't, and if you think you can, you will.' You're going to be the most awesome guest judge they've ever had on *Fashion Showdown*."

Kate's words wrapped Zoey in a warm blanket of reassurance.

"Thanks. But remember, this is Super-Extra Top Secret."

"My lips are zipped," Kate said.

The morning passed quickly, although Zoey had a hard time concentrating. She kept doodling dance dress designs in her notebook and daydreaming about her appearance on *Fashion Showdown*. Even when Mr. Dunn made a comment about her unusual clothing choices, it didn't bother her.

Aunt Lulu once said Mr. Dunn was an "old curmudgeon." Zoey started to wonder what made him that way. She was standing in the lunch line, imagining the tragic story of Mr. Dunn's lost love, when Ivy turned up with Shannon and Bree.

"OMG, what is she wearing?" Bree asked. "Is she trying to be a bumblebee?"

"The shape of that skirt is like a warning sign," Ivy said. "Like, warning: dork approaching."

Bree laughed so hard, she almost dropped her tray. Shannon giggled too.

When people said that names never hurt, they were wrong. Zoey always tried to pretend that the taunts didn't get to her, but sometimes the words stuck in her head and repeated themselves when she was feeling down.

But today was different, because Zoey had the Secret. She might be a dork, but she was a dork who'd been asked to be a guest judge on *Fashion Showdown*. It was *sooooooooo* tempting to casually mention it to Ivy, Bree, and Shannon, just to see the expressions on their faces. But if she did and for some reason the *Fashion Showdown* people changed their minds . . . Ugh, Zoey didn't even want to think of how awful Ivy would make her life if *that* happened. So she just smiled, quietly confident because she knew what she knew.

Zoey's smile wasn't the reaction Ivy expected. She glared at Zoey, then walked past her, as if nothing had happened.

Bree and Shannon glanced at each other, shrugged, than followed Ivy. Bree ignored Zoey completely, but Shannon gave her a curious look, as if she were wondering what was different. Zoey grinned, thinking about the secret glowing inside her like a warm golden flame, and Shannon, startled, scurried off to catch up with Bree and Ivy.

If only she had something like this to carry around inside her every day.

"Did you pass?" Zoey asked Marcus when she got home from school. It was the day both of them had been waiting for: the day he'd take his final driving test. If he passed, he'd have a mostly unrestricted license and could drive without an adult in the car.

Marcus reached into his back pocket and handed Zoey his shiny new license.

"Yay! You did it!" she said, giving him a hug.

"Of course I did! Did my little sister doubt me?"

"No. I knew you would pass."

"I'm putting an ad in the paper tomorrow, warning all the other drivers in town to watch out," their dad said.

"So I better go drive somewhere now before the word is out," Marcus said. "How about it, Dad? Can I take the car for a spin?"

"Yes! I want to go too!" Zoey said.

Mr. Webber sighed. "When did you two get so grown up?" He pulled a twenty-dollar bill out of his wallet and handed it to Marcus, along with the car keys. "Here. Go buy some ice cream for dessert. This kind of milestone requires ice cream."

"Definitely!" Zoey agreed.

"Drive safely. And pay attention to the road," Mr. Webber said.

"I will," Marcus called as he headed out to the garage.

On the way to the supermarket, they had a discussion about what flavor ice cream to get.

"We're celebrating my independence. I should get to choose," Marcus said.

"Okay, but not Chubby Hubby. I don't like that."

"How about Phish Food? Or Late Night Snack?"

"Both!"

"Sounds like a plan!" Marcus declared. "So what do you think? Am I an ace driver or what?"

"Pretty ace," Zoey said. "You'll be even more ace if you drive me to A Stitch in Time when I have fashion emergencies."

"As long as Dad lets me borrow the car and I don't have a hot date."

Zoey sighed. "Ugh. Dates."

"What's the matter? You still haven't asked What's His Name?"

"No. Not yet. Maybe not ever."

"It's like the Nike ad, Zo. Just do it."

Zoey was glad when they pulled into the supermarket's parking lot, since Marcus had to focus on parking. If only it were as easy as just doing it.

They were just getting out when Marcus's cell

phone rang. It was Grace Hone. Zoey had never heard Marcus talk about her.

Marcus handed Zoey the twenty-dollar bill. "You go in—I'll wait in the car," he said.

Did Marcus have a girlfriend he wasn't telling her about?

Zoey headed into the market and straight for the freezer section. She found the ice cream and opened the door to search for the flavors she and Marcus had agreed on, when out of the corner of her eye she caught sight of . . . Lorenzo! He was with his mom, down by the frozen breakfast items. Zoey gazed at Lorenzo through the glass freezer door, which was slowly starting to fog from condensation, all thoughts of ice cream forgotten as she marveled at just how incredibly cute he was. His mother walked into the next aisle and Lorenzo turned toward Zoey's direction. Wait. Was he smiling at her?

Just do it, Zoey thought. *He's on his own, and Ivy isn't here to laugh at me if he says no.*

She took a deep breath and walked toward Lorenzo—SMACK—nose-first into the open freezer door. She let out a squeak of pain and ducked into a crouch, trying to hide from Lorenzo, forgetting that the door, although slightly fogged over, was made of glass, so he could still see her.

Please don't let him have seen me.

There was no way she could ask him now. Not after walking nose-first into a door.

Zoey waited until Lorenzo walked into another aisle, and then she grabbed the Phish Food and Late Night Snack and crept to the checkout, making sure to avoid Lorenzo and his mom. As soon as she'd paid, she ran out to the car and jumped in.

"Quick, Marcus, leave!" she hissed.

"Gotta go," Marcus said into the phone. "See you tomorrow."

Marcus started the engine. "What's the hurry? Did you forget to pay or something?"

"As if!" She saw Lorenzo and his mom coming out of the store. "I'll explain in a minute. Just drive, *please*?"

Her brother shrugged and backed out of the space, slowly and carefully. Lorenzo was walking in their direction. Zoey sank down in the seat so he wouldn't see her. It figured that Marcus would have to drive right past Lorenzo to get out of the parking lot, wouldn't it?

"What's up, Zo? You're acting weird," Marcus asked. "It wouldn't by any chance have anything to do with that guy we just passed, would it? The one who looked in the car?

"He looked in the car?" Zoey groaned. "My life is totally over."

"Yeah. He also waved after we went by."

"Wait—he waved?"

"Yup. And since I have no idea who he is, I have to assume he was waving at you."

"Lorenzo waved at me?"

"If that's his name. Or at least he waved in the direction of our car as it passed by."

"Oh my gosh, Marcus! What do I do? Hold on a minute; let me text Priti and Kate!"

Zoey typed furiously and pressed send.

"So can you tell *me* what this is all about?" Marcus asked. "Is this *the* guy . . . the one you wanted to ask to the dance?"

"Yes! And I was finally going to ask him because

he was alone in the frozen aisle, but then I nose-planted into the door of the ice-cream section! And I think he saw me do it!"

Marcus tried really hard not to laugh.

"Oh, Zo . . . I know it's not funny . . . but it's kind of hilarious."

"It's not! I'll never be able ask him to the dance now!" Zoey wailed. "How will I even face him in class?"

"He waved at you, didn't he?" Marcus said.

"I guess. What if he was just saying 'Bye, Loser'?"

Marcus stopped at the red light. "Sheesh, why are you stressing about this so much, Zo? I never did the date thing in middle school. It's more chill to just go with friends."

"Um . . . could that be because you had the most insane crush on Nicole Doyle and she wouldn't even *look* at you in middle school?" Zoey said.

"Maybe that had something to do with it. Being six inches shorter than her might have also been a deal breaker," Marcus admitted. "But at least I wasn't trying to hide behind see-through doors in the ice-cream aisle."

Zoey had to confess he had a point there.

"But Priti already has a date," Zoey said.

"So? Do you do everything the same as Priti?" Marcus asked.

"Um . . . no," Zoey said. "We're best friends, but we're different."

"So why do you have to have a date just because she does?"

Zoey didn't have a good answer. And just the thought of not having to worry about getting a date for the dance made her feel . . . lighter. It was exciting to imagine what it would be like to go to the dance with Lorenzo, but now that she realized she didn't *have* to get a date, she felt so much better.

Her phone buzzed. It was Kate, telling her not to worry about Lorenzo, she was sure everything would turn out fine. Two seconds later a text came from Priti saying it was a catastrophe and Zoey should call her to strategize the minute she got home.

Zoey set her phone to vibrate. She needed to think.

"I guess I don't," Zoey said. "Maybe I'll still ask

Lorenzo. But whether I've got a date or not, I'm going. Which means I need a dress."

Marcus smiled. "That's more like it."

"So who is this Grace Hone person you're so chatty with?" Zoey asked.

Marcus kept his eyes on the road and said, "Just a girl in my class," but his face turned bright red.

"Sure she is," Zoey teased. "That's why you're blushing."

"Okay, she's a really funny, cute girl in my class, okay?" Marcus said. "But don't tell Dad. One member of my family teasing me is enough for now."

"I won't say a word, " Zoey said. "Can you drive me to A Stitch in Time tomorrow?

"If Dad lets me use the car," Marcus said.

Zoey couldn't wait to get home to her sketch pad and pencils. She had a superawesome dress to design—for herself to wear!

----- CHAPTER 5 -----

Zoey "Nose" Best

Well, despite the fact that I look like Rudolph the Red-Nosed Reindeer's long-lost cousin (long story, but it involves my nose, a door, and ice cream), I've made a decision: I'm going to the dance, even if I don't have a date. (Gasp!) It's funny. You worry about something so much, and then when you decide it's not the end of the world if it doesn't happen, it's like someone just rolled a huge boulder off you and you can start breathing again.

Once I decided to go, the first thing I thought about was designing a fabulous dress. I want it to be beautiful, but something that I feel "me" in. I headed straight to my mom's closet to look for inspiration. She had this really cool velvet dress, but it just doesn't fit right, you know? I guess I could take it in here or there, but I kind of like keeping her clothes just as they were. Maybe I'll grow into it and wear it to my high school prom! So instead of wearing Mom's dress, I'm making my own Zoey-fied velvet dress. Marcus promised to take me to A Stitch in Time to buy fabric as soon as Dad gets home with the car. I can't wait to get started!

In the meantime I'm almost finished with Priti's dress. I'm so glad Jan told me to get the stretch sequin stuff instead of sewing on each sequin individually. I had to do that for the sequins around the hem, and it was really fiddly and took me forever. If I'd had to do the whole dress, I think I'd have graduated middle school before I finished! Whoever invented sequin fabric, I owe you one!

Lorenzo didn't mention their encounter in the frozen aisle when she saw him in school, so Zoey relaxed, figuring that by some miracle he hadn't seen her.

That night Rashida Clarke called to speak to Zoey.

"Hi, Zoey. I wanted to touch base and confirm you're still on?"

"Definitely!" Zoey said.

"Fantastic," Rashida said. "As I explained to your father the last time I called, we'll need you here the night before so you can be here bright and early for hair, makeup, a wardrobe consultation, and a dry run of the judging process."

"That's fine," Zoey said. "Dad arranged for my aunt Lulu to come with me, because it's hard for him to get off during the week. Plus, no offense, it's more her kind of thing, if you know what I mean."

Rashida's laugh was warm and full.

"I understand completely. No offense taken. My father only watches when I'm coming for a visit. My uncle, on the other hand, loves it and watches every episode religiously. Go figure."

"My brother, Marcus," Zoey told her, lowering her voice so Marcus couldn't hear, "pretends to be doing something else, but then he complains when someone gets voted off."

"Well, I'm sure everyone in your house will be giving this episode their full attention," Rashida said. "I'll send you and your father an e-mail in a few minutes with your train and hotel bookings and confirmation numbers, a consent form because you're a minor, and a timetable of our shooting schedule for the day. Now that it's official, feel free to tell people! Great talking to you again, Zoey, and I look forward to meeting you in New York."

"Me too!" Zoey said. "I can't wait!"

Zoey tried to concentrate on her homework, but she kept taking breaks to check if the e-mail from Rashida had arrived. She finished everything except for reading two chapters from *The Misfits*.

She showered, got into her pj's, and decided to check her e-mail one more time before settling down to read. Finally! There was an e-mail from Rashida Clarke!

She and Aunt Lulu were going to take a 1:15 p.m. train to New York next Thursday afternoon. A car would pick them up at Penn Station and take them to their hotel, LM House. The car was scheduled to pick them up at seven the next morning to bring them to the studio. They'd be on set all day and then take the train back at . . .

Zoey's eyes widened in horror when she saw the time of the return train. Six forty-five? The dance started at five, and the ride was more than an hour long! There was no way she'd be able to be on *Fashion Showdown* and go to the dance.

Zoey slammed her laptop shut and threw herself back on her pillows. She'd just been to A Stitch in Time that afternoon and spent her savings on fabric for the dress she'd designed. Would it all be for nothing? It just didn't seem fair.

But as much as Zoey wanted to go to the dance, she couldn't imagine giving up the opportunity to be a guest judge on *Fashion Showdown*. Just thinking about going to New York and getting to meet with real-life designers made her tingle with excitement from head to toe. Giving that up would be hard, and Zoey wasn't sure she wanted to do that.

Sighing, she picked up *The Misfits*. Maybe reading about the problems of Bobby and his friends would help distract her from her own.

As soon as Kate sat next to her on the bus the following morning, Zoey launched into a description of her dreadful dilemma.

"It's so unfair," she complained. "Why does everything good have to happen at the same time?"

"I dunno," Kate mumbled.

Zoey realized that Kate seemed subdued and not her usual self.

"Are you okay?" she asked. "Is something the matter?"

Kate didn't answer right away. She looked down at her fidgeting fingers. Then she looked up at Zoey, her brow creased with worry.

"Oh, Zoey, I feel sooooo bad! I don't know what to do!"

"What is it?" Zoey asked, alarmed.

"So . . . yesterday, after practice, Felix started talking to me. I didn't really think about it much because he's on the team and . . . well . . . he *asked me to the dance!*"

"He what? But he said he'd go with Priti!" Zoey exclaimed. "And it's supposed to be a Vice Versa dance. That's breaking the rules!"

"I know," Kate said.

"What did you say?"

"That's the worst part," Kate groaned. "I knew Priti liked him, but I didn't want to hurt his feelings, so I said I'd think about it. But of course I won't go with him since he said he's going with Priti!"

"I can't believe he even asked you," Zoey said. "That's so wrong!"

"I know," Kate said. "But he did. What should I do?"

Zoey didn't know. The one thing she *did* know was that she didn't want her best friends to fall out over a rule-breaking boy like Felix, who would ask out one girl after saying yes to another.

"I think you should tell Priti what happened, just like you told me. Be honest. And then tell Felix the Faithless that you wouldn't go to the dance with him if he were the last boy on the planet."

"I can't say that!" Kate exclaimed. "It would hurt his feelings."

"Okay, just tell him you have other plans," Zoey said. "But I care more about hurting Priti's feelings. So tell her the truth."

"I will," Kate promised. "When we see each other at lunch, I'll tell her everything."

Libby met Zoey in the hallway after third period. She didn't look happy.

"Did you hear about Kate and Felix?" Libby asked.

Zoey felt sick.

"Hear what?" Zoey asked.

"They're going to the dance together. Felix said he asked Kate and she said yes. I heard him telling all his friends in my last class."

"Nooooo . . ." Zoey groaned. "This is terrible."

"I know," Libby said. "Doesn't Priti like Felix? Why would Kate say yes to him when she knows Priti likes him? That's so wrong."

"She didn't say yes!" Zoey exclaimed. "She told me on the bus this morning."

"So . . . why is Felix going around telling everyone they're going to the dance together?"

Zoey sighed. "Because Kate didn't exactly say no, either. You know what Kate's like, Libs. She got all flustered and didn't want to hurt his feelings, so she told Felix she'd think about it."

"And he decided that 'thinking about it' meant 'yes'?"

"I guess. Which stinks, because Kate was going to explain everything to Priti at lunch, and now she's probably going to hear about it from someone else. . . ."

"And she'll be mad at Kate instead of Felix," Libby said.

"Right. And Felix is the one she *should* be mad at, because he said he'd go to the dance with her when she asked him."

"What? Priti already asked him and he had the nerve to ask Kate?"

"Seems like it."

There was a poster for the dance on the wall

near them. Libby looked up at it. "I feel like taking that thing off the wall and ripping it into a zillion pieces," she said. "I'm starting to wish we weren't even having this stupid dance."

"It'll be fun," Zoey reassured her friend, feeling a pang because she might not be there herself. "We just have to make sure Kate and Priti don't fall out because Felix is being a jerk."

It was too much to hope that Priti hadn't heard the news. The expression on her face as she walked toward Zoey on the way to the cafeteria told Zoey she had.

"I just heard that Felix asked out Kate and she said yes," Priti fumed. "I can't believe Kate would do that—it doesn't seem like her! She *knew* I asked Felix. I texted her about it when it happened."

Zoey really wanted Priti to hear what happened from Kate. She didn't want to be the man—well, the girl—in the middle.

"Priti, I know you're mad. I would be too," Zoey said. "But, please . . . let Kate explain what happened."

"Are you taking *her* side?"

"I'm not taking anyone's side," Zoey said. "You're my best friends, and I don't want you to be mad at each other over something Felix did."

That piqued Priti's curiosity. She had to know what Felix had done, no matter how upset and confused she felt about Kate. She marched over to the table where Kate and Libby were sitting and pulled out a chair, scraping it along the floor with a loud screech, just in case they didn't realize she was mad.

"P-Priti," Kate stammered. "I've been waiting to talk to you all morning."

"Yeah, Zoey told me," Priti said.

Kate blushed miserably.

"I'm so sorry, Priti. I didn't mean for any of this to happen."

"What exactly *did* happen?" Priti asked.

"Last night after practice, Felix came up to me and started talking. I figured it was because I was friends with you," Kate said. "Then, out of nowhere, he asked me to the dance!"

"He what?!" Priti exclaimed. "But . . . he already

said yes to me! And it's a Vice Versa dance. That's breaking the rules!"

"I know, right? That's what Zoey told me this morning!" Kate said. "I can't believe the nerve of that guy."

Zoey was relieved that her friends seemed to be in agreement when all of a sudden Priti said, "But wait—why does Felix think you're going to the dance with him? He's told at least a third of the school you're his date, and it's only lunch."

"Priti, you know me. I'm a total wimp," Kate said. "I just didn't want to hurt his feelings by saying no to his face, so I said I'd think about it. I definitely didn't say yes. I would never do that, because I know you like him."

Priti's brown eyes met Kate's pleading blue ones across the table. Zoey and Libby held their breath, hoping everything would be okay between them.

"I wouldn't go to the dance with that slime, anyway," Priti said. "Anyone who asks out a girl after he's already said yes to another doesn't deserve a date to the dance. I'll tell him that from you and from me."

Kate smiled with relief. "You do that!"

"Can I watch?" Libby asked.

"Me too!" Zoey said.

"Look," Priti said. "This whole date business is causing so many problems—why don't we just forget about it and be one another's dates?"

"That's what Marcus suggested!" Zoey exclaimed. "He said it was more chill that way."

"I'm in," Libby said. "I didn't want to ask a date in the first place."

"Count me in!" Kate said. "I bet you will be better dates than any guy—especially Felix!"

Zoey looked at her smiling friends, feeling torn. She wanted to be part of the "date" more than anything—except maybe being a guest judge on *Fashion Showdown*.

"I might not be able to go to the dance," she confessed.

"What! *Why?*" asked Priti.

"I've been asked to be a guest judge on *Fashion Showdown*, and the taping is the day of the dance," Zoey explained. "It doesn't look like I'll get back in time."

"YOU'RE GOING TO BE ON *FASHION SHOWDOWN*?!" Priti exclaimed. "That's TOTALLY AMAZING!"

"Go, Zoey!" Libby said. "Tell us *everything*! How did they ask you to be on the show?"

Zoey told them about the phone call from Rashida Clarke—the call she thought might have been Lorenzo calling for a date, but wasn't.

"*Fashion Showdown* calling to ask you to be a judge is way better than Lorenzo, if you ask me," Libby said.

Zoey wished she could have had both, but she continued with the story. "So, anyway, Rashida e-mailed the train tickets, and the train back from New York leaves Penn Station at six forty-five, which means there's no way I'll get back in time for the dance."

"Did you tell them?" Kate asked. "Maybe if you explain, you can leave earlier."

"She can't do that!" Priti exclaimed. "This is the big time. It's *Fashion Showdown*!"

"I haven't asked," Zoey said. "I'm scared that if I do, they'll tell me not to come 'cause they'll think

I'm not professional. Just a stupid kid."

"You're not stupid, Zo," Libby said. "We don't think so. All your blog readers don't think so."

Zoey wondered if it was worth asking Rashida if she could leave earlier. Usually, it was so easy to keep everything separate—being Zoey Webber the seventh grader and Sew Zoey the designer. It was the first time she'd ever felt like the two parts of her were pulling her in opposite directions. Why did life have to be so complicated?

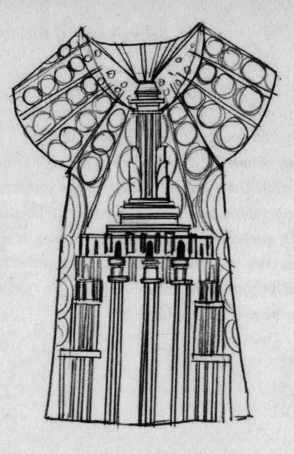

CHAPTER 6

The Amazing Secret: Revealed!

Maybe I'm missing something, but if you ask me, dating seems confusing and complicated. I'm glad the girls and I have just decided to go to the dance as a group. Except . . . I might not be able to go at all.

Do you want to know why? Remember the MOST

AMAZING THING IN THE WORLD I told you about in an earlier post? I can finally spill. Are you ready?

Drumroll

I've been asked to be a guest judge on *FASHION SHOWDOWN*! In New York City! Can you believe it? I still can't. It's probably the best thing that's ever happened to me. How will anything top this?

The only bad part is that I'm most likely going to miss the dance. I know most people would kill to be on *Fashion Showdown*—me included—but I wish I didn't have to choose.

Well, looking on the bright side, I don't have to worry about sewing my dress anymore. But things that happened today reminded me about how great my friends are, so I wanted to make them some accessories to go with their dresses. I got the idea from Frida Kahlo's ribbon-and-flower hair decorations. Now, if I can just make them look like they do in my mind . . . I don't want to say more, in case they're reading this, but I'll post sketches when they're all done. For now, here's a sketch of an outfit I came up with, inspired by New York City, just for fun. Honest truth: I drew it last night to keep me from blogging about *Fashion Showdown*!

"Are you feeling okay, Zoey?" Mr. Webber asked at dinner on Wednesday night. "You've barely said a word. It's not like you."

"Yeah, who are you and what have you done with my sister?" Marcus said. "I'm not used to speaking in uninterrupted sentences."

Even Marcus's teasing couldn't bring a smile to Zoey's face.

"What is it, honey?" her dad asked.

"It's the dance," Zoey said. "And *Fashion Showdown*. And everything."

A tear rolled down her cheek. She wiped it away with the back of her hand.

"Can you be a little more specific?" her father asked.

"You know Rashida sent the tickets?" Zoey said. Her father nodded. "Did you see what time the return train leaves?"

"Six forty—Oh no!" Mr. Webber exclaimed. "That means you'll be too late for the dance."

Zoey nodded miserably.

"That stinks," Marcus said. "After you just

bought all that stuff to make your dress."

"It's not just the dress." Zoey sniffed. "It's my friends. We decided today we were going to forget about getting dates and just go together, like Marcus said. But I'm not going to be there."

Mr. Webber got up. "I'm going to call Ms. Clarke and see if you can take an earlier train."

"No, Dad, don't!" Zoey exclaimed. "What if they say I can't be on the show?"

"I'm just posing the question, Zo. If you can take an earlier train, problem solved. If not, then you haven't lost anything."

"Okay. Call her. Can you do it now?"

"Sure," her dad said. "Rashida gave me her cell number. I'll call her right this very minute."

Zoey couldn't eat another bite of dinner. She was too nervous about hearing the answer to be hungry, and anyway, it would be too hard to hold her silverware with her fingers crossed.

"Hi, Rashida. It's Jack Webber, Zoey's father," her dad said. "No, everything's fine. I was just wondering if I could run something by you."

He explained Zoey's dilemma. "So we were

wondering if there was any way Zoey and Lulu could take an earlier train."

Zoey listened with bated breath as her father said, "Yes. . . . Uh-huh. . . . Yes . . . I understand completely. . . . Thanks, Rashida, it's much appreciated. Zoey's really looking forward to being on the show. Bye now."

"Well? What did she say?" Zoey asked, uncrossing her fingers because they were starting to hurt.

"The bad news is that they really need you on set most of the day if you want to be a judge, which I'm pretty sure you do."

Zoey's heart sank. No dance. No dress. No date with her friends.

"The good news is they'll try to see if they can wrap early so you and Aunt Lulu can catch an earlier train," Mr. Webber said.

"They will?" Zoey said, jumping up and hugging her father. "That's awesome!"

"Zo, don't get too excited. Rashida said she'll do her best, but she can't make any promises. This is a major TV show, and you've made a commitment to be a guest judge. It's a big honor. Part of growing up is about making choices."

"I know." Zoey sighed. "Why does it have to be the same day as the dance?"

"Because unfair, life is," Marcus said in a Yoda voice.

"I just want you to have realistic expectations," her father said.

"I won't get excited," Zoey promised. "I probably won't be able to go, anyway."

She picked up her dinner plate.

"Are you done? You've barely eaten anything," said Mr. Webber.

"I'm not that hungry," Zoey said, and went to the kitchen to drop off her plate.

Up in her room, Zoey stroked the soft velvet she'd bought for her dress. She'd been so excited to create her outfit. Now there was no point. She understood what her father said about making choices. It was just . . . she wished she could have it all.

Zoey folded the fabric neatly and put it back in the bag. Maybe someday she'd have a chance to make something special with it. She decided to bring an old dress to the show in case she made it to the dance, but she wasn't counting on it.

For the next few days Zoey put all her energy into putting the finishing touches on Priti's and Kate's dresses. She brought the dresses to school the following Monday. She was so giddy from seeing the looks on Kate's and Priti's faces when they saw their dresses that she floated through the day.

Gabe tapped her on the shoulder before English, but she barely noticed. "Hey, Zoey . . . ," he said, tapping again. "Have you decided what you're wearing to the dance yet? I need to know so I can get a corsage to match your outfit."

Corsage? Dance? Gabe?

Zoey was confused. Why did Gabe think she was going to the dance—with him?

All of a sudden it hit her—when Ivy had said no one would want to go to the dance with Zoey . . . Gabe had said he would . . . Did that mean he'd asked her? She'd thought he was just being nice. She didn't realize she'd said yes. And now Gabe was looking at her, waiting for the answer about what she was wearing to the dance she couldn't even go to because she was going to be in New York, taping an episode of *Fashion Showdown*.

Zoey wished dances had never been invented.

"The thing is, Gabe . . . I don't think I can go to the dance after all," she said.

Gabe looked taken aback. "Why not?"

"I'm . . . going to be on TV. I've been asked to be a guest judge on a show called *Fashion Showdown*."

"You're missing the dance because you're going to be *on TV*?"

He sounded so incredulous that Zoey wondered if he thought she was making the whole thing up to get out of going to the dance with him.

"Um . . . yeah. They asked me to fill in because the original judge couldn't make it."

"Wow. That's . . . cool," Gabe said.

But Zoey sensed that he was hurt, and she felt awful. He'd stuck up for her when Ivy was being mean, and now she'd made him feel bad, even though she didn't mean to.

"It's one of my favorite shows. But . . . I'm really sorry about the dance, Gabe."

Gabe shrugged. "Whatever. It's no biggie."

Zoey wasn't sure which made her feel worse—hurting Gabe's feelings or having him say it was "no biggie" that she couldn't go with him. Not that she really wanted to go with him. She wanted to go with Lorenzo. But still . . .

Dances definitely should never have been invented.

"I'm thinking about calling Rashida Clarke and telling her I can't do it," Zoey told her friends when they were all seated at the lunch table.

Priti stared at her, sandwich halfway to her mouth. "Can't be a guest judge on *Fashion Showdown*? Are you feeling okay?"

"Zoey, why?" Libby asked. "You've always wanted to visit New York. And it's *Fashion Showdown*!"

"You've got to do it," Priti demanded. "I want to know the inside scoop!"

Only Kate was silent. She'd known Zoey the longest—they'd grown up together, and she knew Zoey wouldn't consider such a thing unless she was really upset about *something*.

"What's on your mind, Zo?" Kate asked.

Zoey explained about Gabe and how she hadn't even realized he'd asked her to the dance. "And now I'm pretty sure I've hurt his feelings because I'm not going, and even though I explained about the show, I'm not sure he believed me. Do you blame him? I'm not sure *I'd* believe me."

"Okay, so you hurt Gabe's feelings. I get that part," Libby said. "But still . . . it's *Fashion Showdown*."

"I know." Zoey sighed. "I guess maybe I'm so confused from trying to be both Designer Zoey from Sew Zoey and just plain old Zoey from Mapleton Prep. Maybe I should just try to be a normal middle-school girl for a change and do what normal middle-school girls do, like go to the dance with her friends."

Her friends exchanged glances and then, to her surprise, they burst out laughing.

"What's so funny?" Zoey demanded.

"Being 'a normal middle-school girl,'" Libby said, using her fingers for air quotes. "I mean, who even knows what that is? You? Kate? Priti? Me? Or maybe Ivy, Shannon, or Bree?"

"But—" Zoey started to protest.

"And another thing, Zoey—there will be other dances," Priti pointed out. "But who knows if you'll ever get another chance to be a guest judge on *Fashion Showdown*?"

"She's right," Kate said. "Remember last year? Everyone just stood around because they were too nervous to ask anyone to dance."

"It's true. It was kind of boring," Priti admitted. "We had more fun at the sleepover afterward."

"Yeah," Zoey agreed. "The dance was kind of lame. But this year we're older. It'll be different. And we've got one another for dates."

"We can take a bunch of pictures for you," Libby suggested. "That way you'll feel like you were there with us."

Zoey hesitated, still torn between wanting to be with her friends and living her dream.

"Zoey, if you don't do *Fashion Showdown*, don't you think you'll always wonder 'what if?'" Kate asked.

Zoey realized her friends were right. There would be other dances. But she might never get another opportunity to be a guest judge on *Fashion Showdown*.

"Okay, I'm going to New York," she said. "But you have to promise to take tons of pictures, okay? And tell me *everything*!"

"We will," Priti promised.

"And you have to tell us everything about being on *Fashion Showdown*," Libby said.

"I will," Zoey said with a grin. "All the juicy details."

After school, Zoey headed to Marcus's room to see if he could give her a ride to A Stitch in Time.

"Sure—just give me a few minutes to finish up this problem," he said, not looking up from his homework.

While she was waiting for Marcus, Zoey experimented with sketches for her idea. She wanted to make the same thing for all her friends, but have each one match her friends' dresses and personalities.

"So what's today's fashion emergency?" Marcus asked on the way to the store.

Zoey explained how she'd been thinking of bailing on *Fashion Showdown* and how her awesome friends made her realize she had to go.

"Whoa! I'm glad the crew talked you out of it," Marcus said. "You love this stuff, Zo. You light up the minute you start talking dresses and design with Aunt Lulu. It's like music for me—or sports for Dad."

"I know. . . . Anyway, I want to make something special for Priti, Libby, and Kate. I've got an idea and I'm hoping Jan can help me with it."

"Well, here we are," Marcus said, pulling into a parking space. "I'm going to get coffee at Roast. Meet me there when you're done."

"Hi, Zoey!" Jan greeted her from behind the big counter in the middle of the store. "What brings you here today?"

"I have an idea for a special present I want to make for my friends," Zoey said. "For the dance— although it out I'm probably not going to be able to go to it after all."

"Oh no!" Jan exclaimed. "After you bought all

that beautiful velvet . . . What a shame."

"The *Fashion Showdown* taping doesn't finish till late in the afternoon, so our train won't get back in time for the dance," Zoey explained. "I thought about not doing it, but my friends talked me out of that."

"Your friends helped you make a good decision," Jan said. "Carpe diem."

"Carpe what?"

"It's Latin. It means 'Seize the day.'"

"So it's like another way to say YOLO?"

Jan laughed. "What's that stand for again? 'You Only Live Once'? I suppose it's the same idea, yes." She settled her reading glasses on the end of her nose. "Okay, show me what you've got in mind for this special present."

Zoey opened her sketchbook and showed Jan the rough sketches she'd drawn.

"Ooh! Pretty!" Jan said. "They're going to be a little fiddly—especially this one." She pointed to the design for Libby. "But I've got an idea to help you make them a little easier."

She took out a pencil and wrote some notes in

the sketchbook for each design, explaining to Zoey how to put each one together.

"Thanks!" Zoey said. "I want these to be really special so my friends know how much they mean to me."

"I think they'll feel very special in these—like royalty, in fact. Let's go find what you need."

Jan came out from behind the counter, and together, she and Zoey chose wire, ribbon, and a selection of beads, rhinestones, and silk flowers.

"You know," Jan said, "it might save time to get some headbands. I don't sell them here, though. You'll have to go to the pharmacy next door."

"That's okay," Zoey said. "I have time, since I'm meeting my brother at Roast whenever I'm done, anyway."

Jan rang up her purchases and put them into a bag. "I hope you plan to blog while you're in New York. It looks like I'm never going to get my chance in the spotlight, so I want to experience the excitement of being on TV through your posts."

"Oh, I'm going to! All my Sew Zoey readers— not to mention my friends—will kill me if I don't!"

Jan came around the counter and gave Zoey a hug, along with her bag of supplies. "Have a wonderful time, my dear. Enjoy every single minute."

"I will!" Zoey said. "And you'll be able to read all about it on Sew Zoey!"

After buying the headbands, Zoey met Marcus at Roast and they drove home. She couldn't wait to get started creating the presents for her friends.

"Hey, Zo, can you get the mail?" Marcus asked when he pulled into the garage. "I forgot to get it when I came home from school."

Zoey walked to the mailbox. Along with the mail, there was a small package addressed to her school address, postmarked from New York City. On the front, there was a note from Ms. Austen, the school principal.

Dear Zoey,

This arrived at school late in the day. It looks like it's from Fashionsista, so I'm dropping it off at your house in case it's something you can use on your trip.

Break a leg, sweetie!
Ms. Austen

Dumping her A Stitch in Time bag and the rest of the mail on the kitchen table, Zoey opened the package. Inside was a tube of clear, expensive designer lip gloss and a card.

Dear Zoey,
Here's some lucky lip gloss for your television debut. I wear the same kind whenever I'm on TV, and it seems to bring me luck. Hope it helps you shine like the star you are! :)
Xoxo,
Fashionsista

Fashionsista's on TV? Zoey thought, more curious than ever about the identity of her fashion fairy godmother. *Wow!* Zoey hugged the card, relieved she hadn't let down Fashionsista by backing out of the show. Not only would she go on *Fashion Showdown*, she was determined to make Fashionsista, Jan, and her family, friends, and Sew Zoey readers proud. She decided to save the lucky lip gloss for the big day. She would need all the luck she could get!

But first she had special gifts to make for Libby, Priti, and Kate to wear to the dance. The rest of the week passed in a blur. Between school and gift-making and packing, she almost didn't have time to freak out! Almost.

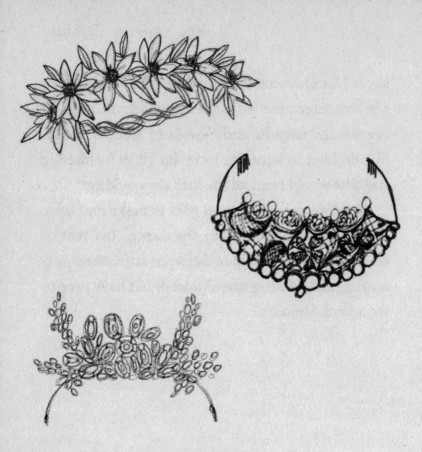

---------- CHAPTER 7 ----------

New York, New York!

TODAY is THE DAY! This afternoon, I leave for THE
BIG APPLE! I'm embarrassed to tell you how many times
I've packed and repacked my suitcase. Okay, I'll tell you.
TWELVE TIMES. I can't figure out which outfits to bring
for *Fashion Showdown*. Rashida Clarke said to bring a

few different choices so the wardrobe consultant can tell me what will look best on TV. I thought I had great clothes, but when it came time to pack, I seriously felt like I had NOTHING TO WEAR. Do you know the feeling?

A big hug and a THANK-YOU to Fashionsista for the lucky lip gloss and the vote of confidence. I hope they let me wear it for the show. It'll make me feel like I've got my Sew Zoey team with me when I'm on camera.

I still feel sad about missing the dance. But I'm soooo excited about the surprise gifts I've made for Priti, Libby, and Kate! Aunt Lulu and I are going to drop these off at their houses on the way to the train station so they'll have them for the dance. I made them promise not to look at today's post. . . . No peeking, girls!

So, here are the final sketches of their gifts. I made them tiara-crown things out of headbands, wire, flowers, and beads to match each of their dresses! Priti's has lots of beads and rhinestones because she loves—and lives—to sparkle. Kate's is more simple, because, well, that's her thing. I thought the daisies would look pretty with her dress. And Libby's has pearls with pink lacy ribbon to match her birthday-cake dress. I'm thinking of the tiaras as hair jewelry to go with their dresses. . . . I really hope they feel like princesses! Get it? I'm *sew* lucky to have them as BFFs!

Well, got to go do my last-minute packing (and check my suitcase one last time!). Sew long for now!

Zoey watched from the train window as the landscape changed from suburban to urban.

"I can't believe we're really on our way to New York City!" she told her aunt Lulu.

"Are you ready for Lulu and Zoey's Big Adventure?" Lulu asked. She reached into her tote bag and pulled out a handful of fashion magazines. "I've got some reading material to get you in the mood."

Zoey looked through the stack. *Vogue*, *W*, *Elle*, *Très Chic*—all her favorites. "I want to read them all. But I have to finish *The Misfits*, because we have a test next week."

She rummaged in her backpack and found her copy of the book. When she looked up, Lulu's eyes were glistening with unshed tears.

"What's the matter?" Zoey asked, alarmed.

"Nothing, sweetie. I was just thinking how proud Melissa would be. I wish she could be here to see what an amazing kid you've become."

Zoey had to swallow to speak. "I wish Mom could be here too," she said. "But since she isn't, I'm glad you are."

Lulu gave her a hug, and Zoey breathed in the comforting scent of the fragrance her aunt always wore.

"I'm honored to accompany you," Lulu said. She leaned back in her seat, got a tissue from her purse and wiped the mascara carefully from under her eyes. "We're going to have a blast in the Big City, you and me, Zo."

Lulu picked up *Vogue*. "Go on, finish your reading, and I'll give you some magazines."

Zoey finished *The Misfits* halfway through the train ride and closed the book with a satisfied sigh.

"That was such a good book. I wonder . . . if maybe, someday, I'll ever be as brave as Bobby."

"I haven't read it. Tell me about it," Lulu said.

"Who is Bobby, and what makes him so brave?"

"He's the Misfit who tells the story. And he's brave because he speaks up against the people who call him and his friends names."

Lulu sighed. "Middle school is tough. There was one girl at my school; I'll never forget her. Marcy Lindeman, who seemed to think it was her life's mission to make me miserable."

"I know what you mean," Zoey muttered.

Lulu looked at her intently. "Has someone been giving my Zoey grief?"

The last thing Zoey wanted to be was a tattletale. She worried that if she told Lulu about Ivy, Lulu would tell her dad, he'd go to Ms. Austen, and things would just get even worse.

"You know . . . kids say stuff," she said, shrugging. "But that's just how it is."

"Just because that's how it is, doesn't mean it's how it should be," Lulu said. "And it doesn't mean you should take anyone giving you a hard time."

"I know," Zoey said. "But it's not like you can do a whole lot about it. I mean, in *The Misfits* they did, but that's fiction. It's . . . different in real life."

"No niece of mine is going to get pushed around without a fight, Miss Zoey," Lulu said, her lips set firm with determination.

It was just what Zoey was afraid of. Lulu was ready to go on the warpath. Next thing she knew, her dad would be on the phone to Ms. Austen.

"It's not that bad, really," Zoey said. "It's just this one girl."

"All it takes is one," Lulu explained. "Marcy Lindeman had enough mean in one pinkie finger to terrorize the entire seventh grade."

"I know, but really, I'm fine. Just don't tell Dad, okay?"

Lulu studied Zoey, looking deep into her eyes. "Okay, Zo. I won't say anything to your dad—for now. But on one condition."

"What's that?" Zoey asked.

"You promise that you'll come straight to me if this person gets out of line. Deal?"

"Deal," Zoey said, breathing a sigh of relief. "Now can you please pass me *Très Chic*?"

When the train pulled into Penn Station, Zoey followed Lulu along the platform into a huge cavernous space. It was overwhelming; so many people moving in different directions, all of them looking as if they knew where they were going, which Zoey certainly didn't.

"Come on, Zo, this way. Our driver's meeting us in front of 2 Penn Plaza."

They walked out of the station's entrance and onto the noisy street, where a few black sedans waited by the curb. One had a white sign with MISS Z. WEBBER in the window. When they walked up to it, a man in a dark suit and chauffeur's cap got out.

"Miss Zoey Webber?" the man asked Lulu.

She laughed. "No, that's my niece. I'm her aunt, Lulu Price, along for the ride."

"I see. Good afternoon, Miss Webber." The man smiled at Zoey. "My name is Winston, and I'll be your driver while you're in New York. Can I take your bag for you?"

Her driver? Zoey couldn't wait to get into the car so she could text Priti, Libby, and Kate.

Winston opened the door to the backseat to let

them in before walking around to the driver's seat.

"Straight to the hotel, ladies?"

Zoey wanted to see the Statue of Liberty, the Empire State Building, and Times Square.

But Lulu said, "Yes, please."

She turned to Zoey. "We can check into the hotel, get settled, and then go do some window-shopping and find somewhere nice for dinner. How does that sound?"

"Fun—especially the window-shopping," Zoey said.

Lulu grinned. "It's pretty exciting, isn't it?"

Zoey nodded.

"So you ladies here for *Fashion Showdown*?" Winston asked. "If you don't mind me saying, you look kind of young to be a contestant, Miss Webber."

"She's not a contestant," Lulu said proudly. "My niece is a guest judge."

Zoey could see the surprise on Winston's face in the rearview mirror.

"You're a judge? Young girl like you? Wow!" Winston said. "I've driven a lot of judges, but you're definitely the youngest."

"Really? Who have you driven?" Zoey asked.

"Let's see now . . . Daphne Shaw, for one."

Zoey almost bounced off her seat with excitement. "Daphne Shaw! What is she like? Is she as beautiful in real life?"

"Yes, she is, Miss Zoey. Tall, too."

"I have to text my friends to tell them that I'm in the same car Daphne Shaw was in!" Zoey said, whipping out her cell phone.

Eventually, Winston pulled up in front of the hotel, a small modern boutique establishment in the heart of Chelsea.

"Here we go, ladies," he said. He got out and held the back door open for them before getting their bags out of the trunk. "I'll be picking you up tomorrow, bright and early at six thirty, to take you to the studio."

Zoey groaned a little at how early she'd have to be up, but she remembered to thank Winston for driving them. She and Lulu walked into the hotel lobby, which had white marble floors and ultramodern furniture. It was like something out of one of Lulu's interior design magazines. She snapped a picture and then texted it to her friends.

Their hotel room was even more amazing. Two queen-size beds with plump white duvets and fluffy pillows, a flat-screen TV, a glass-topped desk with a huge bouquet of flowers, and—

"Look, Aunt Lulu!" Zoey cried. "A gift basket!"

"My goodness! It's enormous! It looks like it's full of swag!" Lulu exclaimed.

Zoey removed the ribbon and tore open the cellophane. The basket contained two *Fashion Showdown* T-shirts, a *Fashion Showdown* tote bag, two I ❤ NY coffee mugs, three different types of cookies, six cupcakes from Magnolia Bakery, a map of New York, a gift card for Blue Bottle Coffee, and four bottles of water.

There was a card nestled inside that read:

Welcome to the Big Apple and Fashion Showdown! See you tomorrow—Rashida Clarke

"It's so nice of her to send us all this food and stuff," Zoey said. "Can I have a cupcake now? This pink one with the white flower looks *amazing*."

"Save it for dessert," Lulu warned. "I want to take you out for a celebratory dinner."

Zoey and her aunt strolled around the neighborhood, checking out stores. To Zoey, the fashions on the street were just as interesting as the window-shopping. New York had an energy all its own, and the people there didn't seem to be afraid to express themselves with their clothes.

"New York's amazing," she told Lulu. "People here don't care about blending in."

"I'm sure some of them still do, underneath," Lulu said. "As I got older, it became easier to relax and just be myself."

As they continued down the block, looking for a good spot to eat, Zoey wondered just how much older she had to be before that happened to her.

After dinner, Zoey stood by the hotel room window, her breath causing condensation on the glass as she watched the city lights twinkling outside. She couldn't believe that she was actually in New York City and that tomorrow she would be the special guest on her favorite TV show.

"Come on, Zo," Lulu said. "We've got an early start in the morning. Time to get into your pj's, brush your teeth, and get some beauty rest."

In the bathroom, Zoey made another exciting discovery. "Aunt Lulu, you won't believe this!" she shouted, toothpaste in her mouth. There's a TV in the mirror!"

"No way!" Lulu called back. She came into the bathroom and found Zoey watching TV while she brushed her teeth. "I stand corrected. Yes, way."

"Isn't it awesome?" Zoey asked, rinsing off her toothbrush.

"Not if it makes you spend more time in the bathroom. Come on now, off to bed. I need to take a shower."

Zoey was too excited to go to sleep. Besides, she'd promised Jan she'd blog about her trip, and she didn't want to forget a thing. As soon as Lulu closed the bathroom door, Zoey jumped out of bed and got her laptop out of her backpack. Leaning back against the pillows, she signed into Sew Zoey.

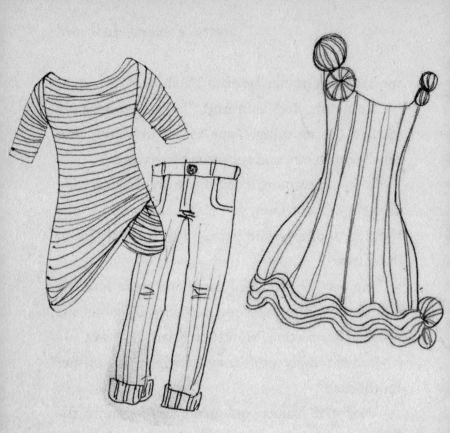

-------- CHAPTER 8 --------

Swagtastic Big Apple!

I'm writing this from my hotel room in NEW YORK CITY! Our hotel room is amazing. There's even a TV in the BATHROOM! Don't worry—New York is much too exciting for me to spend all my time watching television in the bathroom. I could spend hours looking out the window at the people in the opposite building, making up stories about what is going on in their lives. Or sitting at the window table at this little French restaurant where we went for dinner, watching people bustling by. In New York, everyone walks fast, or faster, like they've all got somewhere really important to be and they're running late. When I stopped to look at some sky-high heels in the window of a shoe store, the guy behind us walked straight into me. He didn't even apologize. He acted like I was the one who'd done something wrong! Aunt Lulu said some "New Yawkers" are like that, but it's still her favorite city in the whole wide world.

Guess what was waiting for us in the hotel room? An amazing swag basket of awesomeness! I'm wearing my new *Fashion Showdown* T-shirt to sleep in (comfy!), and I had a s'mores cupcake from Magnolia Bakery for dessert (yummy!).

Here's the clincher: I have to decide which outfit to wear to the *Fashion Showdown* taping. Even though I'm bringing alternates, this is a big moment and I want to put my best foot (well, my best outfit) forward. I brought pieces that can be mixed and matched, so I have options), but that means there are even MORE combinations to choose from! I'm attaching a sketch of my current faves, but when it's showtime I will probably go with whatever the wardrobe consultant likes!

Uh-oh. Aunt Lulu is telling me to turn off the computer and get some sleep. I'm not sure if that's going to happen, though. I'm WAAAAAY too excited!

Zoey woke up before Lulu's alarm went off the next morning. Too excited to lie in bed, she got up and snuck behind the curtains to watch the first rays of sunlight greet the New York City skyline. She couldn't believe how many people were already out and about on the street. *New York really is the city that never sleeps,* she thought.

Today was the big day. Thinking about it made her remember that today was a big day for her friends at Mapleton Prep too: dance day! She rifled through her suitcase to check on her dress—the one she had packed just in case she could catch the earlier train. It was nowhere to be found! Zoey looked through her suitcase one more time.

Her heart sank. How could she have forgotten

to pack her backup dress? If the show taping ended early, if she caught the earlier train, if she made it back in time for the dance . . . she still wouldn't have time to go home to get the dress. Maybe she could wear one of her *Fashion Showdown* outfits in a pinch, she thought, but getting dressed up would be so much more fun.

Zoey's thoughts were interrupted by the sound of her stomach. It was growling, probably from a mix of hunger and nerves. Maybe another one of those Magnolia cupcakes would do the trick. . . . She crept out from behind the curtains and tiptoed over to the desk. With the curtains closed, it was dark in the room and hard for her to see her way around. Zoey had just put her hand on the nearest cupcake when—*Beep! Beep! Beep!*

She dropped the cupcake as Lulu turned on the light.

"Rise and shine, honey—Oh, you're already up!"

"Uh, yeah," Zoey said, her hands behind her back. "I've been up for a little while."

Lulu gave her a half-awake grin. "Go ahead, Zo. A special occasion like this calls for breakfast cupcakes. Just leave room for some protein to keep you going during the shoot. I pre-ordered room service."

Understanding the need for cupcakes for breakfast was just one of the many reasons Zoey loved her aunt Lulu.

Zoey got dressed, but she made sure to keep her alternate pieces in her backpack in case the wardrobe consultant wanted to see them. She couldn't decide how to do her hair, but Lulu told her not to worry, because they would take care of that at the studio. Instead, Zoey put on a beret she had bought from a street vendor on the way to dinner the night before. Zoey had to bring her suitcase to the taping too, because they were going straight from the studio to the train station, and she snuck the unused soaps from the bathroom into her bag as souvenirs.

The room's phone rang after breakfast, just as Zoey was applying a coat of Fashionsista's lucky lip gloss.

"C'mon, Zo—Winston is waiting downstairs with the car," Lulu said.

Zoey took a deep breath, looked at herself in the mirror, and said, "Here we go!"

"Good morning," Winston said as he held open the car door. "How are you feeling this fine morning?"

"Really nervous," Zoey admitted. "I feel like I'm going to throw up."

"I knew I shouldn't have let you eat that cupcake," Lulu said, groaning.

Winston's eyes looked worried in the rearview mirror. "You need me to pull over, just holler."

"I don't mean *really* throw up," Zoey assured them. "At least I don't think so. It's more of an *OMG, I'm about to be on TV in front of a gazillion people* stomachache."

Still, she noticed Winston checking her nervously in the rearview mirror every few minutes, just in case.

When they pulled up in front of the studio, Winston held open the door for them. "Break a leg, kiddo," he said.

"Thanks, Winston. I'll try," Zoey said. "I mean, not to really break a leg, but . . . you know."

"I know what you mean," Winston said, eyes twinkling. "Now, remember the most important thing: Have fun!" Then he tipped his chauffeur's cap and waved good-bye.

Lulu and Zoey checked in at the reception desk and got visitor badges. Zoey took a picture of hers and texted it to her friends. Soon she would actually be on the set!

A production assistant named Sydney came to meet them and bring them up to the studio. Zoey was fascinated by her hair, which was dyed a robin's-egg blue. She could only imagine what Ivy would say if she showed up at school with blue hair. Zoey wished she could ask Sydney if she'd had an Ivy in middle school.

"First stop is makeup," Sydney said, opening a door and ushering them in. "Here we go. Cara will take good care of you."

Zoey sat in one of the makeup chairs, and Lulu sat in another to watch.

"I'm going to make this subtle, so you look natural, but it's probably going to look like a lot more makeup than you would usually wear, especially at your age," Cara said. "How old are you?"

"I'm twelve," Zoey said.

"Wow! And you're a guest judge on *Fashion Showdown*?" Cara exclaimed. "That's impressive!"

"Zoey creates her own designs," Lulu boasted. "She blogs about them on Sew Zoey."

"Wait, *you're* Zoey, from Sew Zoey?" Cara asked. "That's so cool! I read your blog all the time. A lot of us here on the show are fans."

Knowing Cara read her blog gave Zoey the courage to ask the question she'd been dying to ask her.

"So, you know how one of my Sew Zoey readers, Fashionsista, sent me some lucky lip gloss? Is there any way I can wear it for the show?"

Cara frowned. "I'd love to let you wear it, but I have to make sure it works. Can I see it?"

Zoey got the tube of lip gloss out of the side pocket of her backpack.

"Wow, this stuff isn't cheap," Cara said, examining the tube. "This Fashionsista person must really like you. Oh, it's clear. No problem."

When Cara was finished, Zoey stared at herself

in the mirror. She looked like herself, but different. Her eyes seemed to glow, her cheeks were rosy, and her lips shined, as if touched with morning dew.

"You look lovely," Sydney said when she came to get them. "Let's get you down to wardrobe quickly. We're on a strict timetable. We want to help you catch that earlier train."

Zoey had been so excited, she'd forgotten about the dance.

"Oh . . . yes."

Serena, the wardrobe consultant, took one look at Zoey's striped top and told her it was adorable, but much too busy for TV. "Stripes do funny things on camera. What else did you bring?"

Zoey showed her other choices, hoping that one of them would be okay.

"This one," Serena said. "The stars give it some interest without being too distracting."

Zoey got changed quickly, thanked Serena, and then followed Sydney down the hallway to see Brandon, the hairstylist.

"You've got great hair, Zoey," he told her as she took off her beret.

"Really?" Zoey asked. "No one has ever told me that before."

"They haven't?" Brandon ran his fingers through her hair, lifting it up so it fell back onto her shoulders. "Well, they all need glasses."

He brushed out her hair and asked her how she wanted it.

"I . . . don't know," Zoey said. "Whatever you think is best."

"I love this girl!" Brandon told Lulu as he gave Zoey's shoulders a quick hug. "Honey, I'm going to make you look even more fabulous than you do already. How about something like this, so we can see your face?"

He held Zoey's hair up loosely in a high ponytail.

"It's not what I usually do," Zoey confessed. "I like it."

"Oh just you wait . . . ," he said. He got a hair elastic and bobby pins and started brushing. Once Zoey's hair was up, he used the curling iron to perfect the shape.

"Hold on," Brandon said. "I think I have the finishing touch in my magic closet of tricks."

He went to a closet in a corner of the room and rummaged, then came back with something in his hand.

"And now for a finishing touch to the crowning glory!" he announced, holding up a sparkly ribbon to cover the elastic. "Brings out the green in your eyes."

"Perfect!" Lulu exclaimed.

Zoey turned her head from side to side, marveling at her reflection.

"I can't believe that's me," she said.

"It's you, sweetie. You just needed a little something extra to make you sparkle like the diamond you are," Brandon said. "Now off you go to shine on set."

He kissed Zoey and Lulu on both cheeks before they left.

"That was very European," Lulu whispered as they followed Sydney down the hall.

Sydney stopped outside a steel door marked STUDIO TWO. "Are you ready?" she asked.

This was it. The big time. She was about to step onto the set of *Fashion Showdown*.

Zoey's stomach did a somersault, and her mouth felt dry.

"I'm ready," she said, hoping it was true.

When they walked inside, Zoey spotted Oscar Bradesco, the host of *Fashion Showdown*, chatting with the two other guest judges.

"Here's Rashida Clarke, our producer," Sydney said. "I know she's been dying to meet you. She'll introduce you to everyone."

Rashida was tall, thin, and impeccably dressed in a well-cut red pantsuit, accessorized with bold silver jewelry.

"Zoey, so wonderful to finally meet you," she said. "And this must be Aunt Lulu."

"Thank you for the gift basket," Zoey said. "The cupcakes were amazing."

"Life is always better with cupcakes, don't you think?" Rashida asked.

"Definitely," Lulu agreed.

"Let me introduce you to everyone," Rashida said. "We'll be taping in about half an hour."

Zoey surreptitiously wiped her clammy palms on her skirt.

"Oscar, I'd like to introduce you to our very special guest judge, Zoey Webber, and her aunt, Lulu Price," Rashida said.

"Hi, Zoey," Oscar said. "We're so excited to have you on the show. Love your blog!"

Then Rashida introduced her to Christophe Pierre and Aubrey Miller, the two other judges. She recognized them from the pages of *Très Chic*. How was she, seventh-grade Mapleton Prep student Zoey Webber, supposed to be a judge with all these famous people?

"And this is Tom Vincenti," Rashida continued, gesturing to the head cameraman.

Tom smiled and waved.

"You look nervous," Aubrey noted. "Is this your first time on TV?"

Zoey nodded. She didn't trust herself to speak.

"Relax, *chérie*." Christophe told her. Zoey loved his accent. "You will be *parfait*."

"I don't know if I can relax," she confessed. "I kind of feel out of my league."

Aubrey put her arm across Zoey's shoulders and gave her a hug. "Hey, we all were first-timers once.

And I bet if you ask Christophe, he still gets butter-flies before the cameras roll."

"*Oui! C'est terrible!*" Christophe exclaimed. "Yes, I can't count the number of times I have been on camera, but I still get the rumbles in my tummy."

"See? You'll be fine," Aubrey said. "By the way, I love your blog!"

Aubrey Miller read her blog and loved it? Zoey started to relax a little. Everyone was so nice, and they were treating her like an equal, not like a little kid who was invited to guest judge by mistake.

"We're starting in a few minutes," Sydney said. "Lulu, we've got a seat for you behind the cameras, if you'll follow me."

Lulu hugged Zoey. "Break a leg, darling, and remember, 'Fake it till you make it.'"

"I'll try!" Zoey said.

Christophe, Aubrey, and Zoey took their seats in the judges' chairs next to the runway, where Oscar Bradesco was standing in a spotlight. He waited as Jed Fisher, the director, said, "*Fashion Showdown*, episode 201, intro, scene one, take one."

Zoey saw the red lights come on behind the

cameras, and her heart started beating faster. They were taping!

"Our contestants were hard at work most of last night creating designs for our Prom Dress Challenge," Oscar said. "And now they face the moment of truth in front of our distinguished panel of guest judges. Let's meet the panel."

A spotlight shone on Christophe, and Oscar listed his many accomplishments in the fashion field. Zoey panicked, wondering what he would say about her. *Zoey Webber is a kid in middle school who makes dresses in her bedroom and writes a blog. She's only here because our first choice couldn't make it.*

Suddenly, she felt the bright heat of the spotlight on her face and had to try not to squint.

"This week we're especially excited to welcome teen judge and rising design talent Zoey Webber, who writes the popular fashion blog Sew Zoey," Oscar announced.

Zoey exhaled slowly as the spotlight moved on to Aubrey. *Rising design talent Zoey Webber.* Those words were going to be broadcast on nationwide TV. It made her dream for the future seem real.

They took a break for a few minutes before the next take, when the runway show would begin.

"How's it going so far, Zoey?" Aubrey asked.

"Okay," Zoey said.

"You're doing great," Aubrey told her. "Just relax and be yourself."

When the cameras starting rolling for the next scene, Zoey forgot to be nervous, because she was excited to see the designs the contestants had come up with. Each judge had been given a score sheet, and they had to mark the designs based on original-ity, construction, and wearability. There were ten contestants. One design was really cool, but Zoey couldn't imagine dancing in it, let alone going to the restroom. Another one wasn't imaginative, but it was beautifully cut and well sewn. It was the kind of dress that Kate would pick, Zoey thought—one that would look lovely but wouldn't make her stand out in a crowd.

The dress Zoey loved reminded her of the one she'd designed for herself to go to the dance— the one she never finished because she wasn't going. It was velvet, too, with lace inserts instead of zigzags. Zoey wished she could wear that dress to the dance—while dancing with Lorenzo. Sigh.

"Okay, take thirty minutes before we start taping judge reactions," Jed said.

Zoey had been having so much fun, she hadn't realized an hour and a half had passed.

She and Lulu went to the greenroom to get a drink and a snack.

"It's so exciting!" Lulu said. "I'm almost as thrilled as if *I* were on TV!"

"I know!" Zoey said. "I keep having to pinch myself to believe I'm sitting next to Aubrey Miller and Christophe Pierre."

Zoey took out her laptop from her backpack.

"I need to blog about this right away. I don't want to forget a single little detail!"

------------ CHAPTER 9 ------------

Fashion Showdown. For Real!

Imagine getting invited to be a guest judge on one of your absolute favorite TV shows. And then having a professional do your makeup so you look in the mirror and it looks like you but with the zit that was about to erupt covered up and your eyes glowing. And she lets you use the lucky lip gloss that Fashionsista sent you! (Thanks again, BTW!) The wardrobe lady tells you to change your shirt because it's too stripy for TV, but it's okay because you've got another outfit that you both adore. And then the hairstylist tells you have "great hair" and finds a special ribbon in his "magic closet of tricks" that is the finishing touch to the whole thing! But all this isn't even the best part! Because when you walk on the set, you get the best surprise of all—the other judges, Christophe Pierre and Aubrey Miller, are so nice and make you feel like an equal and help you get over your jitters.

I still have to keep pinching myself to believe that I'm here and this is really happening to me. We've taped the first part of the show, and some of the designs are awesome. I can't share anything about them because it's all top secret till the episode airs, but I think it's okay to say that there's one dress I'd LOVE to wear to the dance—well, if I were going, that is.

Oops! Sydney (she's the production assistant) is telling me the break is almost over and I'm needed back on set. More later, during the next break!

Back on the set, Jed explained how he was going to tape the judging segment.

"When you're giving your critique and we come in for a close-up, remember to focus on the contestant, not the camera." He looked at Zoey and smiled. "Just pretend the cameras aren't there."

Zoey looked at the huge TV cameras. Like *that* was going to happen!

"Okay, let's roll 'em. We're going to start with Aubrey, then move down the line."

At least she wasn't going first.

"*Fashion Showdown*, episode 201, judging, scene three, take one."

The camera's red lights blinked on, and Oscar asked Aubrey for her opinion on the first contestant, Christina's, dress, a pink snakeskin-patterned sheath that reminded Zoey of a serpent. Aubrey wasn't crazy about it. Zoey loved how Aubrey criticized the dress without being mean, unlike some of the other guest judges she'd seen on *Fashion Showdown*. Zoey knew how hard it was to come up with designs and to make them without a lot of time to spare. Being a tween designer was like being a contestant on *Fashion Showdown* all the time!

"Now let's ask our special guest judge, teen designer Zoey Webber, of Sew Zoey. Your thoughts on Christina's design?"

Zoey had been so busy listening to Aubrey that she forgot she was up next! When she opened her mouth to speak, *nothing came out*. The spotlight felt unbearably hot, and she could feel her cheeks flushing.

"Cut!" the director shouted.

Zoey wished the studio floor would open and swallow her up as the director strode over to her.

"You okay, Zoey?" Jed asked. "Do you need a glass of water?"

"M-maybe I'm not r-ready for p-prime t-time," she stammered.

"Of course you are," Aubrey said, patting her knee. "It's just your first time on TV. If you weren't nervous, there'd be something wrong with you."

"*Bien sûr!*" Christophe said. "The first time I was on the TV, I couldn't say three words."

"I still get nervous before every show," Aubrey said. "But now I realize my butterflies give me energy if I channel them in a positive way."

"You mean . . . fake it till you make it?" Zoey asked. "That's what Aunt Lulu told me she does when she's nervous about something."

"Yeah, something like that," Aubrey said.

"Try to forget you're on TV," Jed said. "Pretend you're talking to your friends."

"Or the readers of Sew Zoey," Sydney said.

Zoey didn't think she could forget she was on TV. And if she thought about Priti, Kate, and Libby, she'd think about missing the dance. But she *could* pretend she was talking to her Sew Zoey friends.

"I'll try," she said.

"Okay, let's roll 'em," Jed said.

"*Fashion Showdown*, episode 201, judging, scene three, take two!"

Oscar again asked Zoey for her opinion on Christina's dress.

This time she ignored the red eyes glowing above the camera lenses and pretended Christina was a Sew Zoey reader, asking for her opinion. She was honest in her criticisms of the dress, making it clear it wasn't something she'd wear, but she found a few positive things to say, just like Aubrey.

When Oscar moved on to Christophe, Zoey breathed a sigh of relief. Aubrey leaned over and whispered, "Well done. You're a natural!"

Zoey felt like she would explode with pride. She was so glad her friends had convinced her not to give up the opportunity to be a judge on the show. If she had, she never would have met Aubrey Miller, who said she was "a natural." In fact, Zoey started having such a good time once she relaxed that she was surprised when the director yelled "Cut! Take an hour and a half for private judging and lunch."

He walked over to where Zoey and the rest of the judges were standing and stretching, after having been seated for so long. "We've got lunch set up for you in the greenroom so you can decide on the winning designs while you eat. I'll need you back on set by one thirty."

Zoey went to find her aunt.

"You were amazing, hon!" Lulu exclaimed. "A total pro."

"I was sooooooo nervous," Zoey said. "But you were right. I faked it till I made it."

Lulu hugged her. "Told ya, Zo. Never fails."

"Let's go eat," Zoey said. "Now that I think about it, I'm starving."

"It's been hours since breakfast," Lulu pointed out. "It's time to refuel."

"And to pick the winning dress," Zoey said. "I can't believe I get the same say as Aubrey Miller and Christophe Pierre!"

There was a delicious spread laid out in the green-room. Zoey and Lulu filled their plates, and then Zoey joined the other judges to decide the winning dresses. The snakeskin dress was cut right away. When they'd narrowed the field down to five designs, each judge had to pick their winning design and runner-up. Zoey picked the dress she wished she could wear to the dance as her winner, and as runner-up, a peacock-blue silk shift that seemed to shimmer on the model. Christophe's choices were the ones Zoey loved to look at but thought would be really uncomfortable to actually wear. When

Aubrey turned over her choices . . . they were *exactly the same as Zoey's*!

Zoey gasped. Aubrey winked at her and grinned, her teeth pearly white against her red lipstick.

"Great minds think alike, eh, Zoey?"

Zoey was so excited! That meant her favorite dress was the winner.

"We're going to have to keep an eye on this one," Aubrey told Christophe. "She's got a great eye."

"She has to finish high school first!" Lulu warned.

"I haven't even finished *middle school* yet!" Zoey reminded everyone. "Right now, it's hard enough keeping up with homework and my blog. Speaking of which, I need to do another update. I promised I'd write spoiler-free updates all day."

Backstage Pass!

Taping is going well. We're on our lunch break. I'm in the greenroom with the other judges, Aubrey Miller and Christophe Pierre; Aunt Lulu; and Sydney, the production assistant who's been taking us around the studio and making sure we don't get lost. The *Fashion*

Showdown people sure know how to make a girl feel at home—the oatmeal raisin and chocolate chip cookies were almost as good as Kate's mom homemade ones. Almost.

During lunch we chose the winning design and the runner-up, but it's classified information. SORRY! You'll have to wait till the episode airs next weekend. Yes, I know it's not fair, but those are the rules.

Aubrey said I had a "great eye." Can you believe it?! It was like Christmas and my birthday combined!

I was so nervous at first—in fact, when I had to give my first critique, I totally flubbed it and they had to stop filming. But everyone—the director, the producer, and the other judges—they've all been super-understanding and helpful.

I feel so at home with the people here. Not like an outsider at all. It made me think . . . maybe the grown-up world really is filled with misfits like me. Wouldn't that be great?

Zoey's cell phone, which was set to vibrate, buzzed in her pocket as she pushed publish on her blog post.

It was a text from Priti. **URGENT!!! OMG ZOEY! ARE U THERE???**

Yes, I'm here. What's up? Zoey thumbed back.

Just finished gym. Ivy was bragging that Lorenzo asked HER to the dance. ☹, Priti replied.

Zoey felt like her turkey sandwich was about to come back up her throat. It was bad enough she wasn't going to be able to go to the dance. It was bad enough that she never summoned up the courage to ask Lorenzo. It was bad enough Lorenzo never asked her. But . . . to think of him going with *Ivy*?! *Ugh.*

Zo? You still there? Priti asked.

Yeah. Just speechless, Zoey wrote.

Priti's next text was frantic. **You need to come back! Show up in a fab dress! How could he like IVY?!**

Zoey sighed. She wanted to know the same thing. It just didn't seem fair. Ivy was mean to everyone, but the one guy who Zoey had a crush on asked *Ivy* to the dance.

I can't come back. I'm taping Fashion Showdown, remember?! Zoey typed.

Can't they let you out early? Priti wondered.

I don't think so. This is TV, Zoey wrote back.

But this is an EMERGENCY! Priti replied.

Zoey frowned. **Anyway, I don't even have a dress to wear to the dance. I stopped making mine when I realized I couldn't go to the dance, and I left my backup dress at home.**

This is terrible! Priti typed back. **We have to do SOMETHING!** ☹

I don't think there's anything we can do. Just have a good time. And take pics. But NOT of Ivy with Lorenzo. That will make me ☹**,** Zoey typed.

"Time to get back to the set!" Sydney announced.

"Oh—okay," Zoey said. "One sec."

GTG. TTYL, she texted to Priti, and put her laptop and phone in her backpack.

Back on the set, Jed announced they were going to film the judges deliberating in front of the contestants, even though they'd already decided, and then the contestants and their models would come out for one last trip down the runway before the winners were announced. Then each judge would make a comment on the winning design.

As much as she tried to pay attention, Zoey couldn't stop thinking about Priti's text. Why would Lorenzo invite Ivy? It didn't make sense.

"Cut!" the director shouted, startling Zoey.

He walked over to where Zoey and the rest of the judges were sitting.

"Zoey, are you with us? You looked like you were still out to lunch during that take."

"I'm sorry!" Zoey mumbled. "I was . . . distracted."

"Do you need a soda to wake you up? I know it's been a long day, but I need your full concentration."

"No, I'm fine. Sorry."

"Okay, guys, let's take it from the top," Jed said. "*Fashion Showdown*, episode 201, judging, scene three, take three!"

Zoey tried to keep her head in the game as they reenacted the decisions they'd already made in the greenroom.

Focus! she told herself.

But within minutes her brain started drifting to Lorenzo and Ivy at the dance. The two of them slow dancing together, just like she had dreamed of doing with him. . . .

"CUT!"

Uh-oh. Zoey hoped Jed hadn't yelled because of her again.

"Zoey, is something the matter? Because you looked like someone killed your puppy before I called cut."

"I'm sorry. I promise, I'll focus better."

"What's wrong?" Aubrey asked. "You're looking kind of glum."

"*Oui,*" Christophe agreed. "*Tout à fait misérable.*"

"Help us out here, Zoey," Jed said. "You were a total rock star before lunch and now you can't seem to concentrate for more than thirty seconds."

How could she tell them it was about Lorenzo and the dance? They were going to think she was . . . a middle-school girl having middle-school problems, not someone who should be on TV.

"You're going to think I'm silly." Zoey sighed.

Jed raised his hand. "I swear that if you tell me what's the matter, I won't think you're silly."

Zoey gave him a nervous half smile, then took a deep breath and a chance.

"Well . . . it's the dance. The one at school,

tonight. I thought I was okay about missing it—I mean, being on *Fashion Showdown* is such an amazing honor. . . ."

Zoey hesitated, embarrassed.

"But . . . ?" Jed asked.

"I just found out that Lorenzo, this guy I like, asked Ivy, a girl who's really mean to me and my friends, to the dance. It would be bad enough if he'd asked someone nice. But Ivy? It just makes it hurt even more."

"There's not enough money in the world to make me repeat middle school!" Aubrey exclaimed. "I had an Ivy of my own. Meredith Magee. She used to call me Stick Insect, because I was tall and skinny."

"This is not helping Zoey," Christophe said. "We must find some solution for her problem."

"There isn't a solution," Zoey said. "I'm not even *going* to the dance. Our train gets back too late, and I don't have a dress. When I realized I couldn't go, I stopped working on mine."

The other judges exchanged meaningful glances.

"Come on. Let's go find Rashida," Aubrey said. "Relax, Zoey, we've got this in hand."

Zoey sank back into her chair as her fellow judges marched off to find Rashida Clarke. Lulu came over to ask what was happening and why everyone had disappeared from the set. Zoey explained about the text from Priti and how the other judges said they had the situation "in hand."

Lulu looked at her watch. Then she gave Zoey a hug. "Honey, I know it's a big disappointment, both missing the dance and about Lorenzo. But there'll be other dances, and there are definitely other boys. Take your aunt Lulu's word on that. If he doesn't have the good sense to ask out my Zoey instead of some Ivy, he's not worth dating. I don't care how cute he is."

Zoey hugged Lulu back, burying her face in her aunt's shoulder. She knew her aunt was probably right, but . . . Lorenzo? She'd had a crush on him for a long time. She couldn't believe he really liked Ivy.

When she looked up, Rashida, Jed, Aubrey, and Christophe were standing in front of her and Lulu.

"You, my dear Zoey, are looking at your *Fashion Showdown* heroes," Rashida said. "If you can focus for the next hour or so, we're going to do everything humanly possible to get you to the dance on time."

"But . . . the train won't make it on time. . . . And I—I don't have a dress. . . . ," Zoey stammered.

"Trains, *shmains*," Aubrey said. "*Fashion Showdown* heroes don't need *trains*, my dear."

"*Quelle horreur!*" Christophe exclaimed. "*Non! Non! Non!* You will go in a stretch limousine! With a driver!"

Zoey looked over at Lulu, who smiled—and she finally allowed herself to feel hope.

"But . . . the dress . . . ," she said.

"Darling, you can't seriously be worried about finding a suitable dress when you're judging the *prom dress* challenge episode," Aubrey said, smiling. "We've all agreed—you should wear the winning design to the dance."

Zoey couldn't believe her ears. She was going to the dance, in a stretch limousine, wearing her favorite dress!

"We'll send a camera crew down with you to tape your grand entrance," Rashida said. "It'll be the perfect finale to the show."

"Thank you, thank you!" Zoey exclaimed, jumping up and giving each of them a hug. "You really *are* my *Fashion Showdown* heroes!"

"Sydney's going to take you to the workroom to take your measurements," Rashida said. "As soon as we've announced the winner, they can start alterations on the dress. Brandon and Cara have volunteered to go down in the limo with you for last-minute touch-ups. Oh, and I'll need your shoe size."

It was like being in a dream. A magical dream that she didn't want to wake up from, except Zoey knew she wasn't sleeping because soon Ellie, the woman who didn't yet know she'd designed the winning dress, was taking Zoey's measurements.

Ellie's hands were shaking. Zoey wished she could tell Ellie that she had nothing to worry about, but she knew that was against the rules. So she did what the other judges had done for her.

"I'm nervous too," she said. "You saw this morning, right? The first time I had to talk, I couldn't even move my mouth."

Ellie wrote down her waist measurement and

then slid the tape around Zoey's hips.

"You were great," Ellie said. "I can't believe you're only in seventh grade. Promise you'll hire me someday?"

"Only if you haven't hired me first," Zoey said, smiling.

When Ellie had the final measurement, Zoey thanked her and whispered "good luck" before Sydney led her back to the studio.

This time Zoey had no trouble staying focused, because she knew the sooner they finished taping, the better the chance she had of making it to the dance on time. They finished the judging re-creation in one take.

The final five contestants, and the models wearing their designs, walked out onto the runway. Ellie's face was pale, even under the makeup and the spotlights. Oscar Bradesco liked to draw the suspense out for as long as possible. Zoey and Lulu sometimes sat on the sofa at home, screaming, "C'mon! Just tell us who won!" at the TV. Zoey wanted him to make it snappy, and not just to put

Ellie out of her misery. Zoey had a dance to get to!

"And the runner-up is . . . Tony LeSoto, with the stunning blue silk," Oscar announced.

Tony LeSoto and his model embraced, and then he came and shook hands and thanked all the judges. Meanwhile, the other four contestants waited in painful suspense to learn if they were the winner of the challenge or . . . the ones who *almost* won.

"And now the winner of our *Fashion Showdown* Prom Dress Challenge . . . But before I announce the winner . . ."

Zoey could almost hear the contestants' inner groans of frustration.

"There's something special about tonight's winning dress. It's going to be worn by our guest judge, Zoey Webber, to her seventh-grade dance this evening! And our cameras will be there with her. The winner of tonight's *Fashion Showdown* Prom Dress Challenge is"—Oscar paused for dramatic effect—"Ellie Joseph!"

Finally!

Zoey let out the breath she'd been holding and

beamed. Ellie was ecstatic, jumping up and down, hugging her model and then leaping gracefully off the stage to thank the judges. She shook hands with Aubrey and Christophe, but when she got to Zoey, she embraced her.

"I'm so psyched you're going to be wearing my dress to your dance!" she said.

"Me too!" Zoey exclaimed. "I love it!"

"I need to start working on altering that dress if you're going to get to the dance on time!" Ellie said.

"Now, that's a professional," Aubrey said, nodding approvingly as she watched Ellie depart for the workroom. "She just won the biggest competition of her career, but instead of going out and drinking bubbly, she's finishing the job."

As soon as the director yelled "Cut!" and declared it a wrap, the entire staff of *Fashion Showdown* went into action to help Zoey get to the dance. Rashida's assistant brought Zoey five pairs of shoes in her size to try on, each pair more amazing than the next. Lulu nixed the ones with very high heels—Zoey couldn't walk in them anyway, so she didn't mind. They settled on a pair of medium black silk heels with silver soles. Serena, the wardrobe consultant, brought a selection of evening bags and wraps and helped Zoey choose a silver-and-black diamanté clutch and a velvet wrap.

"You are going to look like a million dollars, and that Larry isn't going to know what hit him," she said.

"Lorenzo," Zoey corrected her.

"Whatever his name is," Serena said. "The kid who was dumb enough to ask the girl who gives you a hard time instead of you. And when his eyes pop out of his head like a cartoon character because you look so amazing, I'll be cheering because it'll make up for when Tiffany Taft overheard me talking about the dress I was planning to buy for the senior prom and she went and bought the last one in our size."

It seemed like everyone she met had an Ivy in their lives at one time or another, Zoey thought.

Christophe and Aubrey went to a store near the studio to find the perfect necklace to accentuate the dress. They came back a with a bold glittering drop necklace that was exactly the kind of thing that Zoey would have picked herself.

Finally, Sydney came and told Zoey to come to the workroom for the fitting. Zoey went into the dressing room and tried on the dress. It fit perfectly! It made her feel like she'd stepped out of the pages of *Très Chic*.

"Is everything okay?" Ellie asked. "Does it need adjustments?"

Zoey opened the dressing room door and walked out, head held high.

Everyone in the workroom stopped what they were doing and started clapping. Lulu started crying.

"Zoey . . . Look at you. So beautiful . . ."

Ellie's eyes were glistening too. "I can't think of anyone who could do my dress more justice." She hugged Zoey. "Promise me you'll have an *amazing* time tonight!"

"Thanks," Zoey said. "I will!"

When Lulu and Zoey had thanked everyone at *Fashion Showdown* for the incredible experience and for making going to the dance possible, Sydney and one of the other assistants took them downstairs with their bags to where the limo was waiting.

"Look at the size of it!" Zoey exclaimed. "It's *huge*!"

"They weren't joking when they said 'stretch limo,'" Lulu remarked. "It practically stretches the entire city block!"

The driver got out to open the door for them, and Zoey was thrilled to see it was Winston.

"I couldn't pass up the chance to take Miss Zoey to her dance," he said, winking at Lulu. "You look very lovely tonight, Miss Zoey. And now, your chariot awaits."

Cara and Brandon were already seated inside the limo, which was equipped with a TV, a fridge, disco lights, and a killer sound system.

"Wow!" Cara exclaimed when Zoey climbed in.

"This mean girl Ivy isn't going to know what hit her," Brandon said. "Whatever his name is, he doesn't have a chance, honey."

Cara nodded. "Just relax and enjoy the ride, sweetie. Your *Fashion Showdown* heroes are here to make everything right."

Zoey wasn't sure if they could make *everything*

right. But she was on her way to the dance, in an amazing dress, to hang out with her best friends after spending an incredible day taping *Fashion Showdown*. Maybe that would be enough.

CHAPTER 10

Fashion Showdown Heroes . . . To the Rescue!

I feel like Cinderella going to the ball—except that instead of a fairy godmother I have a team of Fashion Showdown heroes making my dreams come true. And instead of a carriage, I'm in a stretch limo with disco lights, a TV, and Wi-Fi, which is how I can post this while we're on the highway—Cinderella couldn't do *that* in her pumpkin coach. The *Fashion Showdown* people were so totally awesome to make this happen for me—I'd totally given up on going to the dance, and now I'm not only going, but I'm wearing the most gorgeous dress, shoes, and shawl! I can't tell you much about the dress because . . . Well, you'll find out when you watch the show. But I can tell you about the accessories—like my shoes, which have silver soles that make me feel like I twinkle when I walk. And my necklace was a special gift from Aubrey Miller and Christophe Pierre.

Brandon came in the limo with us to do my hair. We decided to put it half up and half down, and then GUESS WHAT?! He pulled out a tiara from his bag of tricks that perfectly matched the necklace Aubrey and Christophe bought. Because they read my blog, they knew about the tiaras I had made for my friends, and they kept that in mind when they looked for the necklace. See what I mean about a team?

Cara's here too, to do my makeup. She is going to make it a bit more dramatic, because it's evening, but I'm going to wear Fashionsista's lucky lip gloss.

Hopefully, it will bring me even more luck!

We're stopping at a rest stop, so, got to go!

Even the best-laid plans can hit horrendous traffic. Soon, Zoey's mood went from excited to anxious. Fortunately, the traffic eased up once they were past some roadwork, and they ended up making good time. They reached the outskirts of town half an hour before the dance. Zoey texted her friends, who were all gathered at Kate's house getting ready so Mrs. Mackey could drive them to the dance.

Have big surprise. I can come to dance!!! Meet me outside in 5 minutes, Zoey texted.

Priti texted back: **OMG what?!**

To which Zoey wrote: **If I tell you what, it won't be a surprise!** ☺

Her friends were waiting outside on the doorstep with the entire Mackey family when the limo pulled up. Zoey could look out, and she could see they were all wearing the dresses and tiaras she'd made for them, and they looked amazing. But with the limo's tinted windows, they couldn't tell it was

Zoey inside until Winston came around and opened the door.

Zoey thought they could probably hear the excited screams back in New York City.

"Oh. My. Gosh!" Priti shouted. "Your dress! It's soooooooo cool!"

"And a limo! I can't believe it!" Libby exclaimed.

"Wait—*we* get to go in the limo?" Kate asked.

"Yes!" Zoey said. "Of course!"

"The lights flash in different colors!" Priti cried.

The girls piled into the limo, and the Mackeys waved them off.

"This is going to be . . . The. Most. Amazing. Thing. EVER," Priti said. "I can't wait to see the look on Ivy's face!"

"I like this girl already," Brandon said. "Come over here and let me touch up your lovely locks."

On the way to the dance, Brandon and Cara put professional touches on Libby's, Priti's, and Kate's hair and makeup.

"I don't just feel like a million bucks. I feel like a zillion bucks," Priti said, looking at herself in Cara's lit-up makeup mirror.

"You all look like a zillion bucks," Lulu said, taking a picture.

Winston parked the limo right in front of the school, and the van with the camera crew pulled up twenty feet behind them. Winston lowered the glass partition between the front seat and the back seat.

"You girls wait in here until the camera crew gets set up so they can film your grand entrance."

"Well, that's our cue to exit stage left," Cara said.

"Our little chickadees look gorgeous," Brandon gushed. "Our work here is done. We'll be in the van with the camera crew if you need a touch-up. Farewell, princesses!"

The girls blew him and Cara good-bye kisses as they exited the limo.

"This is beyond amazing," Libby said, playing with the disco lights. "I could really get used to this."

Lulu laughed. "I wouldn't get *too* used to it. Your stretch limo turns back into a minivan at midnight."

"I know." Kate sighed. "But this is just . . . look! There are Shannon and Bree! They're trying to figure out who's in the limo!"

A small crowd of students had started to gather by the front entrance of Mapleton Prep, watching the film crew set up their gear and speculating as to who was in the limo.

Winston opened his door, stepped out, and poked his head in. "Okay, ladies, crew is set up. I'm going around to open the door for you. Everybody ready?"

"We're *so* ready," Priti said, her voice filled with excitement.

"Have fun, girls," Lulu said. "See you later!"

But Zoey was nervous suddenly—even more nervous than she'd felt that morning before going on camera on the set of *Fashion Showdown*. Sure, she was wearing Ellie's incredible dress, and her hair and makeup were done to perfection. But this was Mapleton Prep, the place where she felt like a misfit.

Winston opened the door, and Zoey was first to emerge from the limo. She heard murmurs of "Who *is* that?" from the students crowded outside the school. As Priti got out of the limo, followed by Kate and Libby, someone said, "Wait, is that

Zoey Webber?" and "Is she some kind of *TV star* or something?"

The girls walked into the building together and headed to the gym, followed by the camera crew, who were trailed by a crowd of curious students.

The dancing had already started. Zoey scanned the room, hoping for a glimpse of Lorenzo. He was on the dance floor, looking amazing in a dark suit with a red tie, but he was dancing with Ivy, who was wearing a dress that was remarkably similar to the snakeskin dress on *Fashion Showdown*, the one Zoey said was her least favorite.

The camera lights went out.

"Zoey," Tom said from behind the camera. "You look like you're having a miserable time. It's not going to make great viewing."

Priti followed Zoey's gaze. "Oh! I see the problem," she whispered to Kate and Libby. "We have to figure out a way to distract Ivy so Zoey can talk to Lorenzo and he can see how amazing she is and fall in love with her."

"Sounds like a plan," Kate whispered back. "But how?"

"I don't know," Priti replied. "I haven't gotten that far yet."

"How about we talk to you ladies about these dresses?" Tom suggested, turning on the camera. "I understand Zoey designed and made them for you?"

"Yes!" Libby said. "We're each wearing original designs from Sew Zoey."

"She made us the tiaras, too," Kate said.

"I've got it!" Priti exclaimed. "Cut! Cut!"

Tom turned off the camera. "I'm the one who is supposed to say 'Cut,'" he said.

"I know, I know. But it's an emergency. I need you to help Zoey have a good time," Priti said.

She explained about Lorenzo and Ivy and asked the camera crew to interview Bree, Shannon, and Ivy about their dresses to distract them.

"If it'll bring a smile to Zoey's face, I'm game," Tom said. "I can't go back with all this footage of her looking miserable. Rashida will have my head."

The camera crew went off to distract Ivy and her friends. Priti tagged along with them.

Zoey was wondering why she'd rushed all the

way back from New York for the dance, just to watch Ivy with Lorenzo and be miserable.

"Hey, how's your head?" someone behind her said.

She turned around to see it was . . . Lorenzo! He looked even more adorable up close than he did from a distance—especially since he wasn't dancing with Ivy. Then it suddenly occurred to Zoey that he was asking about her head, which meant he must have seen her nose-plant into the freezer door the night she saw him in the supermarket. *Awkward.*

"Um . . . fine. Ice cream cures pretty much everything."

Lorenzo laughed. He had the cutest smile.

"So what's with the camera crew following you around? Are you on some kind of reality show?"

"I was invited to be a guest judge on *Fashion Showdown*. I just got back from taping in New York. They wanted some footage of the dance for the grand finale or something."

"Wow. That's pretty cool," Lorenzo said. "You . . . uh . . . look really pretty."

Lorenzo thought she looked pretty! Zoey issued a

silent thank-you to Brandon, Cara, Ellie, and everyone at *Fashion Showdown*. Then she realized she was probably supposed to say something back.

"Um . . . you look pretty too. Wait! I mean—"

"Don't worry." Lorenzo grinned. "I know what you mean. Bet it's been a long day, being on TV and all."

"Yeah, kind of," Zoey admitted. But her day wouldn't be complete unless she danced with Lorenzo. It was a girl-ask-boy dance, wasn't it? Summoning all her courage, she asked, "Do you want to dance?"

"Sure," he said.

They walked to the dance floor just as the DJ switched to a slow song. Zoey was about to ask Lorenzo if he wanted to wait this one out, but he put his arms around her. She put her arms around him tentatively, not really sure where to put her hands. Out of the corners of her eyes, she saw Libby and Kate waving and giving her the thumbs-up.

This was the moment she'd been dreaming about. The moment she'd been waiting for. The moment that was supposed to be the romantic highlight of her evening. She was Cinderella, finally dancing with Prince Charming. Except . . .

"Ouch!" Zoey exclaimed.

Lorenzo had stepped on her right foot.

"Sorry," Lorenzo mumbled.

"It's okay," Zoey said, except her toes really hurt. Meanwhile, she was trying to think of something else to talk about. It felt awkward to just stand there and not say anything.

"So . . . do you like to dance?" she asked him.

Lorenzo shrugged. "It's okay, I guess."

"Ouch!"

This time he'd stepped on her left foot. At this rate, Zoey figured she was going to have to crawl off the dance floor.

"Oops. Sorry."

Zoey didn't think her toes could take another accidental stomp. Dancing with Lorenzo wasn't as wonderful and romantic as she'd imagined it would be. She wished he would say something instead of standing there—and stepping on her toes.

She was relieved when the song ended.

"Well, see you later," Lorenzo said.

"Yeah, okay. See you," Zoey said.

She hobbled back to where Libby and Kate were standing.

"So?!" Libby asked. "How was it?"

"Okay, I guess." Zoey sighed.

Libby and Kate exchanged glances.

"Um . . . you don't sound nearly as excited as I thought you'd be," Kate said.

"I don't know. He didn't talk. It wasn't . . . how I thought it would be."

"Well, my favorite song is playing, so you and Kate should come dance with *me*," Libby said, grabbing Zoey's and Kate's hands and dragging them toward the dance floor. "I promise to keep well away from your toes."

Being on the dance floor with her friends was much more fun than dancing with Lorenzo. For the first time since she'd arrived at school, Zoey relaxed and really began to enjoy herself. She loved the way Ellie's dress swished around her legs when Libby grabbed her hands and twirled her.

As the song was ending, Priti made her way through the crowd, followed by the film crew.

"You won't believe this!" Priti said. "Lorenzo didn't ask Ivy to the dance—*she asked him!*"

"You're kidding!" Kate said.

"I kid you not. It's all on tape," Priti said, nodding to the cameraman. "The crew asked Ivy the story of how Lorenzo asked her to the dance, and she started blushing and stuttering and finally admitted she was the one who asked him."

"But why would she lie?" Zoey wondered aloud. "After all, it's a girl-ask-boy dance."

"Who cares? The point is, you don't have to worry that Lorenzo has a crush on her," Priti announced.

"I don't even want to think about Lorenzo right now. I just want to have fun with my dates," Zoey said. "Come on, let's dance!"

The film crew shot the girls dancing together. When the DJ put on a slow song and they left the dance floor, the cameraman told Zoey, "Now that's more like it. You finally look like you're having a good time."

"I am," she said, putting her arms around Kate, Libby, and Priti. "My friends are the best dates a girl could have."

"Looks like it," he said. "You're lucky."

"I know," Zoey said. "I am."

But then she saw Lorenzo and Ivy slow dancing again, and it still gave her a twinge.

"Hey—do you want to dance?"

Zoey felt a light tap on her shoulder. She turned around and saw Gabe standing there, smiling.

"Oh . . . um . . . sure."

When she walked onto the dance floor with Gabe and he put his arms out, it didn't seem as awkward as it did with Lorenzo.

"So I guess you really were on TV, huh?" Gabe said, with a grin.

"You didn't believe me?"

"I wasn't sure if you were just coming up with an excuse because you didn't want to go to the dance with me. I mean, as excuses go, it was a pretty wild one, but . . ."

"If I was going to make an excuse, I'd make one you wouldn't be able to prove wrong," Zoey said. "But I wouldn't have done that anyway."

"I know," Gabe said. "The whole *being followed around by a camera crew* thing confirms it."

They smiled at each other, and Zoey thought about how much easier it was to dance with him than it was with Lorenzo.

"So how does it feel to be a TV star?" Gabe asked. "Am I going to have to ask for your autograph every time I see you in class now?"

Zoey laughed. "Only on Monday. After that it's back to normal."

"Look, all your friends are out here too."

Zoey looked around, and sure enough, Libby, Kate, and Priti had all been asked to dance. The disco ball hanging from the ceiling flashed hundreds of sparkling moonbeams across the gymnasium floor. The camera lights went on, and she realized this was being filmed for *Fashion Showdown*. She was having her Cinderella moment—just not with Lorenzo.

When the song ended, she thanked Gabe for the dance.

"Hey, have you taken your picture in the photo booth yet?" he asked.

"No," Zoey said.

"Come on. Let's do it," he said, grabbing her hand.

They all ended up trying to squeeze into the photo booth together—four girls and Gabe—and ended up with some *very* funny pictures.

Zoey was sad when the gym lights came on, signaling the dance was over.

"Well, I guess I'll see you on Monday," Gabe said. "Don't forget—I want your autograph."

"You got it!" Zoey said.

Winston was waiting outside with the limo. Zoey said good-bye to the rest of the *Fashion Showdown* crew, who were heading back to New York in the van.

"Thank you for everything! You guys are the best!" she declared.

"We're glad you had a good time," Tom said.

"And Mean Girl Ivy knows who's the *real star* of this school!" Brandon said.

"I have to get this guy back to New York," Cara said. "He's a bad influence. Bye, honey!"

The girls waved at the *Fashion Showdown* van and then piled into the limo.

"Did you young ladies have a nice time at the dance?" Winston asked.

"It was the best!" Priti exclaimed. "So much better than last year."

"Magical." Zoey sighed.

"You were the best dates ever," Kate said.

"Definitely!" Libby agreed.

Winston put on music, and they sang the entire way back to Zoey's house.

Mr. Webber made the girls pose for picture in their dresses before their parents came to pick them up.

Priti begged Zoey to tell them more about her trip. "We want to hear the stuff you didn't put on your blog. All the *juicy details*."

Zoey started to tell them about her adventures, but as the energy from the dance gave way to her exhaustion from the long day, she began yawning.

"I want to hear all about New York too, but Zoey is tired," Mr. Webber said. "It can wait until tomorrow."

Zoey tried to protest, but she yawned again instead. Finally, she said, "I'll call you," and she stumbled upstairs. She promptly fell asleep, still wearing her dress and tiara.

------------ CHAPTER 11 ----------

Not a Dream, a Fashion Fairy Tale!

Have you ever had the kind of magical evening where you're having so much fun, you don't want it to end, ever? That was last night. Thank you, THANK YOU to everyone at *Fashion Showdown* for helping me to get to the dance. You are the best fashion superheroes!

lights, camera, fashion!

Imagine showing up at the school dance in a suuuuuper streeeeeeeeeeeetch limousine, followed by a film crew. It definitely made us the center of attention—something I'm not used to being every day. Well, any day!

What were the best parts? Let's see . . . Dancing with my dates, Libby, Priti, and Kate. Slow dancing was fun too—but my favorite slow dance wasn't with the guy I thought it would be with; it was with someone else. Weird, huh? Oh, and trying to squeeze five people into a photo booth for funny pictures. Coming home to see Dad and Marcus, who I missed while I was in New York. Eating Dad's pancakes in the morning. I even guessed the secret ingredients (marshmallows and Nutella and chocolate chips) on the first try.

If I watched a TV show about what happened this weekend, it would seem too good to be true—going to New York, being a guest judge on *Fashion Showdown*, meeting Aubrey Miller and Christophe Pierre. Thinking I was going to miss the dance, but then having the entire *Fashion Showdown* team make it work so that I could go in amazing style! I guess it proves that magic really can happen—if you've got good friends.

Oh! I know you've been asking for pictures of the dress, but I still can't show you. You'll have to tune in to *Fashion Showdown* next Friday at eight p.m., when ALL WILL BE REVEALED!!! I'll be watching in the comfort of my living room. My friends are coming over for a screening pajama party. It's going to be SEW MUCH FUN!

Everyone was sitting on the couch in front of the TV—in their pajamas—waiting for the commercials to end and *Fashion Showdown* to begin. Even Zoey's dad was wearing pajamas!

"Hurry up with the popcorn, Marcus," Zoey called. "It's about to start!"

"Just because you're on TV, doesn't mean you can turn into a diva," Marcus said as he came into the living room carrying two huge bowls of steaming buttery popcorn.

"Let her play diva tonight," Lulu said. "But *only* tonight."

"It's not every day you're on TV," Mr. Webber agreed.

"I know, I'm really proud of you, Zo. Would I be wearing these if I wasn't?" Marcus asked, pointing to his pajamas. Somehow, he had found footed pajamas—the kind that look like a baby's onesie and zip up in the front—covered with neon guitars and music notes.

Everyone laughed, but Libby laughed so hard, she almost started to cry. When she could speak again, she explained, "Oh my gosh, Marcus. I've been trying not to laugh, in case they were your favorite pajamas or something!"

"Thanks, guys, I needed a laugh! I'm so nervous," Zoey said. "What if I sound like an idiot, with gazillions of people watching?"

"You won't!" Kate assured her.

"I was there, remember?" Lulu reminded Zoey. "And at no time did you sound like an idiot—except when you couldn't speak at all, and I'm sure they edited that out."

Zoey laughed and threw a popcorn kernel at Lulu. "Thanks a lot!"

"Quiet! It's starting!" Priti exclaimed.

All eyes were glued to the television as the

Fashion Showdown theme song played during the same opening sequence Zoey had watched so many times before. But now that Zoey had actually been there, it looked different. She knew how many people were just off set, working to make the program run smoothly.

Oscar Bradesco introduced the contestants and the challenge—and then the camera moved to the judges. There she was! But what had seemed like forever during the taping turned out to be only a second or two of screen time during the actual show.

"Wait! That's it?" Priti said. "You were only on-screen for, like, thirty seconds!"

"I don't care," Zoey said. "As long as I wasn't saying anything dumb."

"So far so good," Marcus said. "But there's still twenty minutes left in the show."

Zoey knew he was just teasing her. Marcus had been just as excited to watch the show as she was.

But the rest of the program had been heavily edited too. After the long day spent on set—the hours of taping after overcoming her nerves and doing lengthy critiques of each dress—each of her responses were cut to about a sentence. And the whole segment at Mapleton Prep lasted all of one minute—just a visual of Zoey walking into the dance in her dress with her friends and then a brief snippet of them dancing together. All in all, Zoey's time on-screen during the entire episode of *Fashion Showdown* added up to a grand total of three and a half minutes.

But it didn't matter. When the final credits rolled across the screen, everyone in the Webber living room stood up and gave her a standing ovation.

"You were *amazing!*" Kate exclaimed. "I don't know how you got the courage to do that!"

"I'm so proud of you, Zo," her dad said, coming over and drawing her into a huge bear hug. "You were a real pro!"

"Yeah, sis!" Marcus said, rubbing Zoey's head affectionately. "Who'da thunk?"

"I knew you'd be awesome," Priti said. "Because you just are."

"I'm saving my dress forever," Libby said. "So

that when you're a famous designer, I can say I own an original Zoey Webber."

"Stop, you guys," Zoey said. "Or I really *am* going to turn into a diva!"

"Don't worry," Marcus said. "I'll be here to keep *that* from happening."

"Seriously, though . . . I really love New York and all, and I can totally see myself living there someday. . . . Like, when I'm a grown-up and stuff," Zoey said. "But for now, there's nowhere I'd rather be than right here."

Her father and her aunt Lulu had to find tissues suddenly. Zoey went to each of them and gave them a kiss on the cheek.

She didn't notice Priti, Libby, and Kate disappearing into the kitchen.

"SURPRISE!" they said, coming out with a cake in the shape of the dress Zoey wore to the dance. It had CONGRATULATIONS TO ZOEY, OUR FASHION STAR! written on it in gold icing.

"You're a star," said Libby, "but you're also the best friend ever!"

The following Monday at school, Shannon sidled up to Zoey while she was getting books out of her locker.

"Hey, Zoey—I saw you on *Fashion Showdown*," she said, looking around anxiously, as if she were worried Ivy or Bree might see her. "You were awesome. It must have been so cool to be on the show."

"Yeah, it was," Zoey said. "It was amazing."

"Just . . . be careful. *Some people* are really jealous, even though they'd rather cut off their arm than admit it," Shannon said, her voice so low, it was almost a whisper.

"Okaaay," Zoey said, not sure what to make of what Shannon was telling her, especially when she said, "Well, later," and walked off quickly. She assumed Shannon meant Ivy and wondered if Shannon was warning her that Ivy was up to something.

Zoey shrugged. She'd just be on her guard and face whatever came. She wasn't going to let Ivy or anyone get her down.

When she walked into English, her classmates started clapping. It took Zoey a moment to realize they were applauding for her.

"Great job, Zoey!"

"You were amazing, Zoey!"

"SO COOL!"

It was like she'd gone from nobody to some-body overnight, just because she'd been on TV. Kids who'd never paid much attention to her before were smiling and wanting to high-five her as she walked by to get to her desk. Zoey was surprised that it didn't feel good. Instead, it felt . . . strange.

Especially when she saw Ivy, sitting on her hands, making it clear *she* wasn't clapping.

"Hey, how does it feel to be Mapleton Prep's TV star?" Gabe asked when she sat down.

"Really weird," Zoey confessed. "Do you think that's weird? That it feels weird?"

Gabe chuckled. "No, I don't. I'd think it weirder if it didn't feel weird."

Zoey breathed a sigh of relief. "Oh good. I was starting to think I was crazy or something."

"I . . . hope you . . . um . . . . don't think I'm crazy

if I tell you I . . . uh . . . had a great time dancing with you the other night."

Gabe was blushing as he said it, and Zoey felt her cheeks start to flush too.

"Oh . . . no . . . I mean, no, you're not crazy. I did too."

Gabe smiled, his face lighting up. Zoey was relieved when Ms. Brown started class, because she wasn't sure how she felt. She'd had a crush on Lorenzo for so long, but her dance with him hadn't been like she'd imagined. Gabe was nice and fun but . . . she was confused. It didn't make sense she'd had so much more fun with the guy she didn't have a crush on than with the one she did. Maybe she just wasn't ready for dating and boys and all the stuff that went with them . . . yet.

The one thing that did make sense was Sew Zoey. Ever since her visit to New York, Zoey was bursting with ideas for new designs. She couldn't wait to finish her homework every night so she could take out her sketchbook and transfer the images she saw in her head onto the smooth white pages.

Her readers seemed to love them too. And not just her usual fans—ever since the *Fashion Showdown* episode aired, her blog was getting more hits than ever. The traffic counter was practically spinning out of control. One thing was clear—ready or not, Sew Zoey was hitting the big time!

Want to know *sew*
much more?

Here's a sneak peek at
the next book in the
Sew Zoey series:

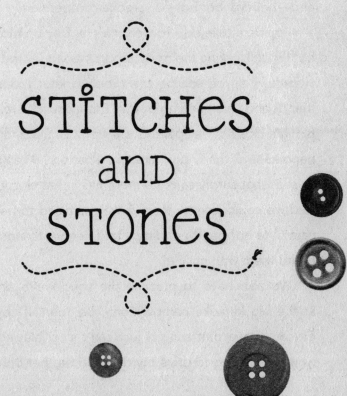

STITCHES
AND
STONES

Woo-hoo for Spirit Week!

Spirit Week is coming up at Mapleton Prep, and I can't wait! Every day has a different dress-up theme, so as you can imagine, it's right up my alley. There's Hat Day, Twin Day, Backward Day, Decades Day, and School Colors Day, so I've been sewing up a storm, working on outfits for the week. On Friday there's going to be a Spirit Assembly with awards for the most creative costumes and—believe it or not—a karaoke competition!

I made a tulle skirt to wear for Hat Day on Monday, but I'm still lacking the most important part . . . the HAT! Hopefully, I'll be solving the problem later today. My friends and I are heading over to Priti's house to raid her family's closets. Her parents are from England, and as her dad says, the English are "mad hatters." I can't wait to see what surprises Priti's mom has in her closet. She said we could borrow them if we promised to be *very* careful to not get them dirty. I told her not to worry; I'll guard them with my life!

We also have to practice the song we're singing at the big karaoke competition: "Be Yourself" by Las Chicas. I love that song; I just can't stop playing it— which is starting to drive my dad and brother bonkers.

Since I'm the only girl in the house, sometimes I feel the need to stake out some territory (even if it's just by playing ubergirly bubblegum pop songs on repeat)! Besides, I'm just getting in the spirit for Spirit Week!

"So do you all have the Spirit?" Priti Holbrooke asked her friends Zoey Webber, Kate Mackey, and Libby Flynn as she opened the front door to let them into the house. She was wearing a huge hat that bore a remarkable resemblance to one of the fancy flowerpots Zoey's aunt Lulu bought for her decorating clients.

"Well . . . definitely not as much as you have," Zoey said. "Where did you get the flowerpot?"

Priti laughed. "It's Mom's. She wore it to my uncle's wedding."

"Doesn't it give you a headache?" Kate asked.

"No," Priti said. "But it's hard to see out from under it. And forget trying to kiss people. I think they made up air kisses because of hats like this."

She pretended to kiss Zoey on either cheek.

"Help me! I'm being *hat*tacked!" Zoey laughed.

"Wow, I want to see the rest of the hats," Libby exclaimed. "But . . . I'm hoping there are a few that are a little . . . um . . . smaller?"

"No worries," Priti said. "There are plenty to choose from. Come on, let's go hat hunting!"

The girls traipsed up to the Holbrooke's spare room. The closet doors had already been flung open, revealing stacks of hatboxes as well as hats piled one on top of the other on shelves.

"I wish people wore hats more here." Zoey sighed. She lifted one of the hatboxes off the pile and opened it. Inside was a white fascinator, which was constructed to look exactly like a sprig of orchids at their most beautiful stage of flowering. "I mean, look at this. It's . . . perfection!"

"Oooh!" Libby squealed, "Can I try that?"

Zoey had been hoping she could wear it, because it would look amazing with the tulle skirt she'd made, but she said, "Sure," and handed it to Libby, who slid the combs carefully into her short copper hair, arranging the fascinator at a jaunty angle.

"What do you think?" Libby asked.

"You look amazing!" Kate exclaimed.

The fascinator really *did* look great on Libby. And there were still plenty of unopened hatboxes.

Priti opened another hatbox and pulled out a pink woven straw cloche with a delicate half veil held in place by a small cluster of pearls and feathers. "Kate, this is *so* you."

Kate didn't look quite so sure it was her, but then Kate wasn't nearly as fond of clothing as she was of sports. "It's really pretty, but . . ."

"Go on, try it on!" Libby urged her, the orchid on the fascinator bobbing with enthusiasm.

Kate plopped it unceremoniously on her head.

"Fashion heathen." Priti sighed and arranged the hat properly, pushing Kate's hair back from her face and straightening the veil. Priti examined her handiwork. "Much better."

"What do you think, Zo?" Kate asked.

"Priti's right, Kate. It's looks gorgeous on you."

"Definitely," Libby agreed. "I love the half veil."

"Okay, okay. I'm sold," Kate said.

"Now we need to get you and Priti hatted up," Libby said.

"Fear not! The Holbrooke Hattery is not

exhausted yet," Priti said, reaching for a hatbox.

Libby took off the lid of a nearby hatbox and pulled out a retro looking pillbox hat with a veil held in place in front with a huge white bow. "I think I like this one almost as much as the fascinator," she said, trying on the pillbox.

Zoey picked up the fascinator and tried it on. "What do you think?" Zoey asked her friends.

"It suits you too!" Kate exclaimed.

Even though she also loved the pillbox hat, Libby looked a little disappointed.

"How about we wear each hat for half the day then switch at lunch?" Zoey suggested.

"That would be awesome! I like them both so much it's impossible to choose," Libby admitted.

"What do you think of this for me?" Priti asked. She was sporting a navy blue wide brimmed hat with an angled crown, decorated with cream-colored flowers.

"I definitely vote that over the flowerpot hat," Zoey said. "We can actually see some of your face."

"And you can kiss us—or anyone else who might be kissable," Libby said, blushing.

"As if!" Priti said.

"And the color suits you," Kate said.

"Okay, well now that our hat choices are settled, we need to practice our karaoke song," Priti said.

"Um . . . I've been thinking. How about I cheer you on from the sidelines?" Kate suggested.

"But it's the grand finale," Zoey prodded.

"I know but—it's a competition."

Maybe it was from years of playing sports, but Kate usually played to win.

"No buts!" Priti said. "Everyone has to be a part of it. We're not just friends—we're a *team*. Besides, I'm working on the most *amazing* dance routine. Here we go. . . ." Priti put her mp3 player into the speaker dock and pushed play and started showing them dance moves.

Zoey watched her friend's feet carefully and tried to imitate her. But she found herself distracted by the noise that suddenly started coming from downstairs. . . .

CHLOE TAYLOR

learned to sew when she was a little girl. She loved watching her grandmother Louise turn a scrap of blue fabric into a simple-but-fabulous dress, nightgown, or even a bathing suit in an instant. It was magical! Now that she's grown up, she still loves fashion: it's like art that you can wear. This is her first middle grade series. She lives, writes, and window-shops in New York City.

NANCY ZHANG

is an illustrator and an art and fashion lover with a passion for all beautiful things. She has published her work in the art books *L'Oiseau Rouge* and *Street Impressions* and in various fashion magazines and on websites. Visit her at her blog: www.xiaoxizhang.com. She currently lives in Berlin, Germany.